And God Belched

Rob Rosen

Copyright 2018 by Rob Rosen

Published by
MLR Press, LLC
3052 Gaines Waterport Rd.
Albion, NY 14411

Visit ManLoveRomance Press, LLC on the Internet:
www.mlrpress.com

Cover Art by Winterheart Design
Editing by Amanda Faris

Print format: ISBN# 978-1-64122-084-2
eBook format available

Issued 2018

Trademarks Acknowledgment

The author acknowledges the trademark status and trademark owners of the following wordmarks mentioned in this work of fiction:

Gerber/Haagen-Dazx: Societe des Produits Nestlé S.A. (Nestle)
Safeway: Albertsons Companies, LLC
Pepto-Bismol/Mr. Clean: Proctor & Gambal
TMZ: EHM Productions, Inc
US/Enquirer: American Media Inc
People: Time Inc.
Rolling Stone: Rolling Stone
Out: Here Media Inc.
iPad: Apple Inc.
Band-Aid: Johnson & Johnson Consumer Inc.
Tag Heuer: TAG Heuer
Disney: The Walt Disney Company
Amazon: Amazon.com Inc
Energizer Bunny: Energizer
Pixar: Pixar
Hallmark: Hallmark Marketing Company LLC
Auto-Tune: Antares Audio Technologies
L'Oréal: L'Oreal Group
Skype: Skype
Wonder Bread: Flowers Foods
Cap'n Crunch: Quaker Oats Company

Dedication

For Kenny, my entire universe—plus any others that might be floating nearby

Chapter 1

In the beginning, God created the heaven and the earth. And the earth was without form, and void, and darkness was upon the face of the deep. And the Spirit of God moved upon the surface of the waters, and God said, "let there be light," and there was light.

Um, you know, sort of.

Actually, in the beginning, God belched out a universe—a big bang of a belch, in fact. It was, so it's told elsewhere, an odoriferous, gaseous cloud of a rumbling belch. And like all good belches, it was followed by several smaller ones, each forming their own universes, which spread out and filled that above-mentioned void.

Ours was belch number four, the very last one. God had to pound his expansive chest to get that one out. "*Oomph,*" He said as our existence was made manifest, as our atoms spread outward, trailing those other far greater universes, just before that famous light was flicked on.

Click.

Picture, if you will, four bubbles floating through the blackness, turning end over end as they rapidly grew and expanded, as molecules collided and elements formed: hydrogen and helium and lithium— so that many years later we could have zeppelins and balloons and long-lasting batteries, and all because God was a bit gassy one day.

Anyway, that first belch, that first universe, went to the right; we veered leftward. Those other two, well, they're not really pertinent to this story. So, for the sake of argument, let's just say that one went up, the other down. Ta ta, sister worlds. Live long and, um, prosper.

A year went by, two, then fourteen billion, give or take. I, too, was made manifest: Randy—both a name, namely mine, and an apt adjective. Made, in fact, by my mom and dad, belching my way into the void on a cold January morning. Yep, just like it's said, we truly are made in His image, at least in belching ability.

In any case, on that same January morning, in a universe far, far away—sort of, though, uh, not really—another baby boy was born: Milo. Well, that's what I called him, anyway. Or at least would, at a time when those two universes happened to decide to play bumper cars together. In any case, his real name was close to a dozen letters long, strung together with nary a vowel to be had. I tried to pronounce it once and was instantly stricken with a sore throat.

But wait, I'm getting ahead of myself here.

Back to me, Randy—the name, for the time being, not the adjective. I was born in San Francisco, the city by the bay, the city by the gays. I lived high upon a hill, one of the steepest in the city, sort of like a prince in a castle. Though our home was made of steel, not brick, not wood, not even stone. The architect was hoping to design a quakeproof house, or so the legend went. And like so many legends, such was not even close to the actual case, as it turned out. Anyway, we froze in the winter and melted when the sun poked through the endless fog. In other words, our house was wisely one of a kind.

"High upon a hill lives Prince Randy, clad in his ermine cape and golden crown, scepter raised in royal salute." The story rolled off my mom's tongue as she fed me Gerber's mashed peas: my favorite.

FYI, the cape was my blankie, not ermine so much as polyester. The crown was a yellow bowl bought at Safeway. I still own said crown. Now I use it for cereal, as opposed to headwear. The scepter was my rattle. It was bequeathed to my younger brother a couple of years later. These days, I lift my cell phone in royal salute.

"Prince Randy will be king one day. Prince Randy will marry a beautiful princess and live in an even bigger castle on an even higher hill, and will live happily ever after."

It was a short story, but, to be fair, it wasn't that big a bottle of

Gerber's. Also FYI, I would become more queen, so to speak, than king. And as for marrying a beautiful princess, yeah, good luck with that. And what of the even bigger castle on the even higher hill? Wait, just wait for it. Oh, and as to that happily ever after, that also remains to be seen.

For now, back to Prince Randy.

I dropped the scepter. My crown tumbled to the floor. I spilled cereal on my ermine cape. I cried like a baby—mainly because I was a baby. You could say that I was a clumsy one, but the dropping and tumbling and spilling were due more to living in an earthquake-prone city than mere childish clumsiness. You could say that, and most people, like the morning news, would've believed you, but, as it turned out, the earth wasn't quaking at the time so much as colliding, all bumper-car-like. And no, no one would've believed you if you suggested such a thing, myself included. That is, until it was me suggesting such a thing—here, in fact.

Mom scooped me up as the ground beneath us trembled and shook. She ran to the nearest doorframe and crouched down, covering me protectively with her body. "*Shh*," she said. "Don't cry, Randy. Those are just friendly giants on their way to say hello, bigger than even the Transamerica Pyramid. *Boom* they go as they clomp their way up our hill."

I shrugged and stopped crying. I suckled on a teat for comfort. It wasn't an affectation that would follow me into adulthood. Dare I say, duh. Anyway, the earth eventually stopped rumbling. The giants returned home—those San Francisco hills too daunting, apparently, even for the likes of them. Mom put her boob away. And I, I was already fast asleep, dreaming of that happily ever after that may or may not be at the end of all this.

§ § § §

Life rolled along. Mashed peas were replaced by whole ones. My blankie became threadbare, until not even my younger brother, Craig, wanted it. The teat was shelved—*phew*—and replaced by whole milk. I stopped wearing a cereal bowl on my head, at least in public. But the ground, yes, the ground continued to shake, rattle, and, you know, roll.

"Strangest thing," said the morning news, which was the only news my mom watched, mainly because she was too tired at night to bother with it. Again, "strangest thing," it said, "but there doesn't seem to be any fault movement during these quakes." It was, as if, there was effect without cause. "And the quakes are only happening in and around the San Francisco area."

"Weird," said Mom.

I shrugged. "Weird," I echoed. I was eight at the time. I was at that aping stage. If Mom said, "Weird," I said, "Weird." If Mom laughed, I laughed. If mom dressed in a dress, I dressed in a dress.

"It's just a phase," she whispered to Dad when I emerged from her bedroom in one of her blouses, teetering in her high heels, my lips smeared in red, eyes in shimmering blue.

I shrugged. "If you say so."

The ground again shook. She ran over and scooped me up, Dad close behind, Craig along for the ride, until all four of us were huddled beneath the narrow doorframe.

"Weird," Mom said.

"Weird," agreed Dad.

But *weird* didn't even begin to cover it.

§ § § §

I went from being eight to fifteen. I went from being short to medium-tall. Heck, I was taller than my mom already, but had a ways to go to beat Dad. Craig was a late bloomer. Craig was adorably scrawny. Thin and short with glasses, he was nerdy chic—his words, not mine. He'd just turned thirteen, his voice alternating from high to low and back again. He sounded like a record repeatedly sped up and slowed down—Mom's words, not mine; mainly because I hadn't a clue what a record even was.

I stopped eating peas. I stopped eating vegetables, altogether. I ate meat. I ate fried food. I was a rebel, albeit one with teenage acne, owing mostly to all that fried food and meat I was forever eating. I grew my hair long. I grew a beard. Or at least I drew one on my face, which Mom promptly washed off. I stopped wearing her blouses. Turned out, it really was just a phase. Go figure. I still wore makeup, though. Just a bit of black smudged around the eyes. Mom let me keep that. Then again, I'd used a permanent marker, so what choice did she have, really?

"What's got into you these days, Randy?" she asked.

I shrugged. I trembled. Actually, the earth trembled. By then, we'd stopped huddling beneath the doorframe. The morning news stopped reporting on it. We stopped calling it weird. The only thing that didn't stop were the quakes themselves.

As to what had gotten into me, it was the quakes. I was certain of it. The earth shook, awakening something deep inside me, something foreign. I felt tied to them, like the ground was putting on a show just for me. It quaked and I grew taller. It quaked and I grew randy—the adjective, not the name, namely mine. So, like I said, *it* had gotten into me. And I, I promptly spewed it out. *Pft, pft, pft* I went, the bathroom door locked, pajamas bunched around my ankles.

"Hormones," my Mom called it, though I, of course, knew better.

§§§§

Fifteen turned to eighteen turned to twenty-two. I was six feet and some change by then, just out of college and still living at home. Mom had mentioned giants when I was a kid. Now, I was the giant. My acne cleared up. My chest filled out. My hair was Sampson-like. I looked like the cover model of a Harlequin novel, only gayer. Mom said I looked like Fabio. I took her word on it, seeing, like records, I hadn't a clue who or what a Fabio was.

I often stared at myself in my standing mirror. It wasn't out of vanity—mostly—so much as fascination. Who was this man staring back at me? Where had he suddenly come from? I felt eighteen inside my head, fifteen, eight, but the person staring back at me was not any of those people.

I bounced my dick. It waved back at me. "Hi, Randy!" it seemed to say. "Let's play!"

I nodded my head. "Good idea, dick," I said, quickly stroking it to climax.

It remained resolute. "Let's play some more, Randy!"

"Really?" I asked it. "So soon?"

It shrugged as it leaked, as an opalescent bead dripped to the floor below. "Sure, why not!"

Why not, indeed.

And it was then, as I came for the third time, as the earth began to quake beneath my already quaking legs, that I saw it for the very first time. I froze, mid-stroke, jizz splattering against the mirror before slowing sliding down. My eyes went wide. I shook my head—the big one, not the dripping littler one. I blinked. I blinked again. "Can't be," I said as I squinted into the reflection, as I moved my face closer to the surface. I chalked it up to coming too many times in rapid succession. My brain was addled. It was a mirage. Too much, uh, *heat*. That had to be it, I told myself.

Eyes, after all, didn't stare back at you from inside a mirror, especially eyes that were a stunning shade of blue.

Oh, and, by the way, mine were brown.

The earth stopped shaking. The eyes disappeared. My dick was still hard as granite. I looked down at it. "Did you see it, too, dick?"

It didn't reply. It was a very single-minded dick. It only wanted to play. Strange mirror sightings, it seemed, weren't its thing. I suddenly blushed and covered my prick. Could the eyes see me? I chuckled nervously. This was crazy. I was seeing things and talking to my dick. It had to be those hormones again, I figured. If they raged when I was fifteen, twenty-two must've been one hell of a bonanza.

It was then I realized that I hadn't locked my bedroom door. I say this because one minute it was closed, and the next it was open, my brother gazing at me as I in turn gazed at him.

"I'm sorry!" he shouted, covering his eyes.

"Craig!" I in turn shouted, further covering my still-turgid tool. It took two hands. I say this out of modesty and not vanity. Again, mostly. "Shut the door! Shut the door!"

He peeked from between his fingers. "Which side should I be on?"

I sighed. "The inside."

"The inside of your bedroom or the inside of the hallway?"

My sigh repeated. I bent down and grabbed my T-shirt, which I wrapped around my waist as best I could. I again stared at my covered-dick, now turned pup tent. Like all good things, my third sigh, like my coming, came, no pun intended, in threes. "Inside my bedroom."

He shut the door, his eyes still covered. "Can I look now?"

I nodded. "Sure, but straight ahead. Down, not so much."

Slowly, he removed his hand from his face and locked eyes with me. "You should lock your door, Randy."

Again, I nodded. "Duh, Craig." I paused. I gulped. "I, uh, I saw something."

He grimaced as his eyes momentarily wandered to my still-tenting equatorial region. "Tell me about it."

"No," I said, turning as I pointed to the mirror. "In there." My gulp repeated. Mainly because I'd also forgotten that there was a rather large spunk-trail still gradually making its way down the glass. And so, I again grabbed my T-shirt, wiped the spooge away as best I could, then found my underwear, which I yanked up and on. The tenting, suffice it to say, remained, but had at last began to abate.

Craig sat on my bed. "If this is some sort of sex education talk, Mom and Dad already have it covered." He pointed at my midsection. "And better than you do."

My blush returned. "Sorry, little bro, it's just...I really did see something."

He looked at me incredulously. "In the mirror?"

"In the mirror."

He nodded. He rolled his eyes. He was apt to do that when he was agitated with me. Which was more often than not. "In the mirror?"

I nodded. "In the mirror."

"Are you on drugs, Randy?"

My nod turned shake. "Mom and Dad would kill me."

He wagged his finger at the mirror. "Yeah, they wouldn't be too thrilled about this shit either." He yawned. "Makes three of us." He fell backward onto the bed and stared at the ceiling. "Though, I am glad you're two years older than me."

"Why is that?"

He turned his face my way. "So I can learn from your mistakes, many and varied that they are."

I grinned and tossed my T-shirt into the hamper before slipping into some shorts. "Lesson one: lock the door."

He nodded from his prone position. "Check. Got it." He pushed himself up onto his elbows. "As to the mirror, those were your eyes. A mirror reflects an image. You were staring at the mirror, as is evident in what Mom will surely find in the hamper. Ergo, those eyes were yours."

"Ergo?"

"Hence. Thus. It's a word, Randy," he said.

"The eyes were blue."

He blinked. "Yours are brown."

"*Ergo*, the eyes weren't a reflection." I closed the gap between us and sat on the bed next to him. "It's the earthquakes."

"What's the earthquakes?"

"It's tied to the earthquakes," I replied. "The eyes." There was silence in the room as he seemed to take this in. "Sounds crazy, huh?" I finally said when I could no longer take the deafening hush.

"Yep." He pushed himself up even further, his back again at the vertical. "Why do you think that your sudden hallucinations are tied to the earthquakes?"

"I wasn't hallucinating." *Was I?* "And as to the earthquakes, I…I don't know. It's just a feeling I have. It's like, it's like they're tied to me, to the eyes." I balled my hand into a fist and placed said fist against my chest. "I feel it, Craig. In here."

He touched his index finger to my temple. "It's more up here I'm worried about."

"I'm not crazy." *Was I?*

"Oversexed, then."

I nodded. Yes, there was that. There was always that. Seriously, always. "Think that's it? Hormones, like Mom is always saying?"

"It's just an educated guess," he said. "Maybe you've reached some sort of threshold. Maybe this is simply a side effect. Maybe leave your willy alone for a while, then the eyes might go away."

I would've agreed, but my willy had a mind of its own, and the little head seemed to rule the big one these days. Not that the little head was all that little, mind you, but still. "I'll try."

He grinned. "I suspect a resounding failure in that regard."

My grin matched his. My brother and I were polar opposites. We didn't think alike or look alike or act alike, but our smiles were strangely identical. "Yeah, probably." I stood. "Don't tell Mom and Dad, okay?"

"About which thing?" He pointed to me, then to the hamper, and, lastly, to the mirror.

"Any of it."

He shrugged and also rose. "Trust me, it's not a conversation I want to have. For a second time. Heck, I could've lived without the first one."

He turned to leave. "Wait," I said. "What did you want when you came in here without knocking first?"

He scratched his head and squinted my way before replying. "Oh, yeah. Almost forgot." His grin amped up a notch. "Mom said to wash up for dinner." His finger rose and again aimed for the hamper. "Pizza. And I'm *so* not touching the slices next to yours."

I chuckled. "I don't blame you, little bro," I said. "I don't blame you one bit."

He turned to leave, while I, in turn, turned to the mirror. "Please," I said in a hushed whisper. "Please don't fuck with me anymore."

And, as if in reply, the ground once again began to shake.

I ducked beneath the doorframe, old habits seemingly returning. Thankfully, the eyes didn't do the same. Return, I mean.

At least not that time.

Chapter 2

Days went by. I left my dick alone.

Okay, let me rephrase that: I left my dick alone when I was anywhere near a mirror. Because, like I said, little head, big head, not so little, *yada, yada, yada*. And those old habits I mentioned did indeed die hard. Emphasis on the hard. Plus, my dick was a rather social creature. In other words, it didn't like to be left alone. To add a plus to that plus, I also figured that I'd need my dick somewhere down the line, somewhere not so sadly solo, and so I thought it best not piss my dick off. Let's call it hedging one's horny bets.

Still, curiosity had a stranglehold on my cat. That is to say, the earthquakes had me wondering. What were they? Why were they so frequent these days? And what was my connection to them? Mostly that last thing.

I knocked on Craig's door. I heard him unlock it before said door opened. "Randy," he said by way of greeting.

"Locking the door?"

He smiled. "I always learn from your mistakes."

"Not your own?"

He shrugged. "If I had any, I'm sure I'd learn from them. As it is, you have enough for the both of us. Maybe that's why Mom had me: to even things out."

I stood there, arms akimbo. "Are you done insulting me now?"

He seemed to think about it, then replied, "For the time being." The door opened wider. "And to what do I owe the pleasure?"

I walked inside. I closed the door behind me. "The earthquakes."

He frowned as his eyes, as usual, rolled in and out like the ocean at high tide. "Oh God, not that again."

I jumped on his bed. His blanket had the Periodic Table of the Elements splashed across it. His desk lamp was fashioned from a large beaker. Einstein stared down at us from above the bed, his tongue forever sticking out. Yes, my brother was a nerd to the pth degree, surpassing nth by two steps. If he ever landed a girlfriend, he was sure to be the most pussy-whipped man on the planet. Still, at eighteen and about to start college, he was the smartest person I knew, which was possibly sad and most definitely true.

"What do you know about the quakes, little bro?"

He sat down in front of his computer and swiveled his chair my way. "Do you want the official word or the chatroom one?"

"There a difference?"

He nodded vigorously. "Night and day, dude. Night and day."

"*Dude*?" I grinned his way.

"I'm trying it on," he said. "How's it fit?"

"Like ten pounds of potatoes in a five-pound sack."

"That bad?"

I shrugged. "It'll grow on me," I replied. "Now, back to the quakes."

His nod returned in full force. "I've been researching it after… well, after the other night, when you were—"

"Never mind that," I interrupted him with. "What did you find?"

He smiled. He clearly loved having this over on me. Brains always trump brawn at the end of the day. I bet that Einstein poster of his outsold Michael Jordan's ten to one. In any case, he leaned back in his chair. He looked like a scrawny Justin Bieber—or maybe make that scrawn*ier*. "The news says that there's no real cause for all this. At least most of the time. It's like the earth is shifting, even when the faults aren't." His smile widened. He could've given the Cheshire Cat a run for its money. "An anomaly, they say. Must be a reason, but one that science hasn't come up with yet. Like maybe an Earth's core issue. Maybe a gravitational one. The sun, the moon, something yanking on us."

I leaned in, my heart pounding, mouth suddenly Saharan. "But?"

"But," he echoed, "only in San Francisco? How can that be? A problem with the earth's core, or with the sun, the moon, that would affect the entire planet, or at least a greater swathe of it."

My stomach tightened up into so many knots that it would take a team of Boy Scouts to untie it. "I'm...I'm in San Francisco."

He laughed. "It's not always about you, *dude*." He winced. "I'm not sure I like it. Sounds forced."

"How about fella, guy, man?"

His wince winced even wincier. "I'm already nerdy enough without calling you *fella*." His mouth shrugged. "Dude. For now, we'll go with that. Lesser of all evils."

I blinked. I'd temporarily forgotten why I was there. Walking into Craig's room was like walking into Tangentland. I shook my head. I remembered. "The chat rooms. What do they say about the earthquakes?"

"Two camps," he replied. "The first ones are the bible-thumpers. This is San Francisco, after all. Your people abound here. God's wrath, they say."

Yes, Craig knew I was gay. Yes, everyone knew I was gay. Mainly because I told them all that I was gay when I was seven. Or at least inferred it.

We were watching a rerun of *Will and Grace* at the time. I pointed at Jack on the screen. "I can relate," I said. Mom and Dad nodded knowingly. The matter was closed. No drama, for which I'd eventually become famous for. No tears, for which Mom was already famous for. No lectures—yeah, see Dad. Craig looked up at me from the floor. "Told you so," he said to my parents. So yes, it seemed I was the last to know. Even a five-year-old had come to the conclusion before I had. Then again, even at five, Craig was extraordinary.

"And the other camp?" I asked, pretty sure it wasn't God being pissed off at us. I mean, why would he put the gays in the most beautiful city in America if he didn't love us so much? Why not put us in, say, Des Moines? And trust me, no one is leaving their heart in Des Moines. No one is wearing flowers in their hair in Des Moines.

"Aliens," he replied.

"Illegal aliens? Like from Mexico?"

He pointed up. "Aliens. From up north. Not from down south."

"Canada?" I was confused. Par for the course.

He sighed, eyes arollin'. "From space, fella." He stared off into the distance, a frown quickly appearing. "No, definitely not fella." He turned to me again. "From space, dude." He sighed. "It'll have to do."

"You could simply call me by my name."

"Dude sounds cooler. And I need all the help I can get."

I nodded. *And then some.* "Anyway, how are aliens causing earthquakes? And why? And why here?"

He shrugged. "Chatrooms aren't exactly known for their depth and breadth of data. Mostly, it's screwballs and teenagers and conspiracy theorists, or a combination of all three. Aliens were suggested; aliens were latched onto. Seeing as there isn't a scientific explanation, it's better than nothing. Besides, an advanced race could cause such an event. Maybe they're testing a new app. On us." He shrugged. "Or maybe it is God. I mean, look at all that shit he pulled in the Bible. Plagues and locusts and frog-storms."

Suddenly, I remembered the eyes. Did God have blue eyes, like in the paintings? Was God watching me masturbate? Repeatedly. Was I God's HBO? Or was it those aliens on the other side of my mirror?

In any case, what Craig had said and what the reality of it all actually was were two entirely separate things—separated by a mere mirror, sure, but still.

§ § § §

I went back to my room and grabbed a chair, which I set in front of my mirror. I inched in as close as I could get to it. "Are you there, God? It's me, Randy." I waited, heart pounding, but there was still no answer, no eyes of searing blue. Still, I reasoned, God had spoken through a burning bush in the middle of the desert, so why not a mirror in the hills of San Francisco? "A sign, God. Give me a sign."

They say that God works in mysterious ways—like a tomato being a fruit. Pretty mysterious stuff, if you ask me. But the fact that I asked for a sign and the earth immediately began to shake, well now, that surpasses the tomato thing by a mile. That's like God slamming down an ace over your king—or, as was the case, *queen*.

I clutched the chair as my teeth rattled inside my mouth. The floor beneath my feet was dancing without a single note of music. My mirror vibrated. I stared into it, into the eyes that soon appeared.

"God?" I rasped.

The eyes didn't so much as blink.

"Martian aggressor? Plutonian attacker? Um, Uranus invader?" I giggled at the double-entendre.

FYI, yet again, my own anus had yet to be invaded. I mean, I hadn't even kissed another guy yet. Oh sure, I lived in San Francisco, and also oh sure, I'd been out for years and years, but I was waiting for Mister Right. Something inside me told me that a special person was out there somewhere, looking for me, while I in turn was waiting for him. I knew it. I felt it. In my head. In my heart. Heck, even my dick knew it, try as it might to argue the point.

All that is to say, I was still a virgin. And if God was about to saunter me through his pearly gates, or the aliens were about to dissect me, with or without a preferably enjoyable anal probe, I was having none of it.

Which is why I covered the mirror with a pair of jeans. "Sorry, God, but I'm not ready for you just yet. Maybe in another eighty years, give or take." *Take* being optimal.

The earth stopped shaking. The floor settled. The mirror stood still. I, on the other hand, was still trembling. I waited for a moment. I waited some more. I counted to ten, twice. When I got to twenty, I kept going, figuring that even God got bored, aliens as well. I mean, how long can you stare at denim before you call it a day? Even Levi Strauss had a hobby, or so I'm guessing.

In any case, hand unsteady, I eventually grabbed my jeans between thumb and forefinger. The material slipped to the carpet, which, by the way, was pink. I picked it out when I was seven. I was making a statement at the time. Too bad said statement was this: Pepto-Bismol rules!

But back to the mirror.

The eyes were still there, even though the earth had already quieted down. Suddenly, I knew what a moth felt like when it encountered a flame. Meaning, though terrified, I couldn't look away, not again. And so, I stared directly into the eyes, into the sea of blue, which I felt like I was drowning in.

"Can you see me?" I hazarded to ask, my voice sounding hoarse. "Blink once for yes, twice for no." The eyes blinked once. "Really?" They blinked again. "Can you hear me?" They blinked twice. "Are you, you know, *God*?" Again, they blinked twice. *Phew*. Thank, you know, God.

"Are you an alien?" The question came out in a whisper, my eyes wide as I asked it, legs madly bouncing all the while as I sat there and waited for a reply, as my mouth summarily dried up. Cotton balls, in fact, were far dewier.

The eyes stayed open. Had he...um, she...um, it...understood the question? "Are you from a different planet, somewhere far out in the universe?" And still the eyes stayed open. What gave? I mean, it was a simple yes or no question, wasn't it? And then it hit me. "From a...a different universe?"

The eyes slowly blinked once. It was as if the owner of the eyes was answering yes, but hesitantly. More like a maybe than a yes. But what did that mean? *Maybe* he, she, um, it, was from a different universe? What the fuck?

Anyway, since this line of questioning wasn't getting me anywhere, I decided to move on. "Can I see more of you, more than just your eyes?"

The eyes blinked. The eyes blinked again. Bummer. "No?" Two more blinks. "So, no." I sighed. "Why not?" The eyes simply stared. "Yes or no only, huh?" One blink.

This was frustrating. I needed help. I needed…"Craig!"

I turned to go and get him, but he was already standing in the doorway. He looked frozen, like he'd just run into Medusa and was unlucky enough to be in her line of sight.

"I didn't lock the door again, did I?" I asked.

His head moved from left to right and back again.

"Say something, little bro."

"Eyes," he squeaked out.

I hopped up. "You see them, too?!"

He nodded, if just barely. "God."

"Nope," I replied. "I asked. Not God. Alien. I think."

He blinked. "You think?"

I ran to the door and dragged him in. He might've been stone, a la post-Medusa, but he was still small and runty. In other words, dragging him was easy enough, the stone more like a pebble. So, in he flung, the door promptly closed behind him. I placed him in front of the mirror. "Ask him or, um, her, or, uh, it, a yes or no question. Yes gets one blink; no gets two."

He looked at me. He looked back at the mirror. He moved his jaw around, apparently trying to break the curse of the snake-headed Gorgon. He inhaled. He coughed. He squinted at the mirror, into the pools of blue. "Are you from this universe?" There were two blinks. "A parallel universe?" There was one blink, a pause, then two blinks.

"There!" I shouted. "I asked a similar question and got a similar answer. Like the alien is saying maybe yes, maybe no. What does that mean?"

He strummed his tiny fingers on his tiny, dimpled chin. He turned to me and stared, clearly deep in thought. "The alien isn't in a parallel universe, not overlapping ours," he eventually replied. "That would mean, if I'm not mistaken, that his world exists, not parallel to ours, but separate, on our timeline, but not in our space." He again turned to the mirror. "Does that about cover it?" There was one blink. Craig snapped his fingers. "See," he said. "Easy."

I coughed. "Easy? Are you insane?"

His shrug reshrugged. "I'm talking to a mirror, so yeah, maybe."

"But how can an alien in a different universe see us and blink at us? And how can it do it through a mirror? And why can we only see its eyes?" I pointed at said eyes. "It told me, in no uncertain words—or any words, for that matter—that all we can see are its eyes. Why is that?"

Again, Craig strummed his chin and again stared at the mirror. "Your mirror, it's a portal of some sort, a window, something connecting its universe to ours, its dimension to ours."

I hated calling the alien an it, by the way, but what did I know? Was it a he or a she? In its universe, was there even such a thing? Maybe it was both, maybe neither. Was it good or evil? Did it want to kill me, be friends with me, mate with me? And yes, even in times of potential peril, I was still randy—the adjective, not my name. Hence the whole mating thing. I mean, it was my mirror we were communicating through, was it not? Well, communicating*ish*, we'll say.

"Fine," I said, "but why can we only see its eyes?"

His chin strumming picked up steam. His chin strumming could've fueled a paddle boat, in fact. Still, eventually, he came up with, "If you stare directly into a mirror, what do you see?"

I shrugged. "Whatever is reflecting off that mirror. So?"

He smiled and slowly lifted his hand, his index finger pointed out, until the tip just barely grazed the mirror's surface. "Yeah, but if you reposition the mirror," he said, pushing his finger forward, "you see more of the reflection, or at least a different angle."

The mirror then did, as he'd said, reposition, while we, in turn, gasped in unison.

"He," I said. "*It* is most definitely a *he*."

Chapter 3

He, in fact, looked like me. That is to say, he looked very Harlequin-cover-model-like, with long blond hair, an aquiline nose, those aforementioned eyes of blue, and cheekbones that Vogue would've photographed for days, given the chance. And since I could now see more of him, he could now see more of me. Or at least I reasoned as much, considering he was smiling in response to Craig and my smiles, nodding as Craig and I nodded. Heck, he even gasped when Craig and I gasped, much like a reflection would, but only slightly off-kilter.

Still, all we could see was his face. Everything else sort of blurred around the edges, became my room. I lifted my hand in front of my face and waved. He did the same. He had five fingers, five manicured nails. I lifted my other hand and waved. He did the same. No wedding ring, by the way—and yes, I was checking. Then again, who knew if such a custom was even practiced on his planet, in his universe. Maybe they didn't marry there. Maybe, heaven forbid, they didn't mate. Or maybe they mated and killed, very black-widow-spider-like. Or maybe, again heaven forbid, he didn't want to mate with me, wasn't even gay. Cart before the horse, though, right? Heck, the horse was so far behind that it might as well have been in the cart with me, coasting downhill. I mean, we couldn't even communicate. I could barely see the smallest portion of him. Was mating even an option? And why was I even thinking such a thought?

Ah, because there was that whole connection I'd felt, felt all along, ever since the earthquakes had started. When I looked into his eyes, the connection was even more palpable, like a tether was binding us together, yanking him to me, me to him. In a mirror, you see yourself, but now, in my mirror, I saw *us*. So yeah, the cart was before the horse, but at least the horse was still in the race, so to speak.

"Weird," Craig said when at last he'd come to his senses.

Me, no, no senses. Not yet. "Which part?"

He grinned. "All of it, but no, that's not the weird I was referring to." He glanced my way. "The alien is in a different universe, but he looks just like us."

"Mostly like me," I made note.

Craig exhaled sharply, eyes rolling like always. Nope, no moss ever collected on those squinty peepers. "Must you?" he asked.

I smiled and nodded. "I must. And your point?"

He shrugged. "Not sure, but like I said, weird. I mean, what are the odds that beings who live, theoretically, millions of miles apart, would look so similar?"

"Similar to me, you mean."

"Again?"

I nodded. "It bears repeating." Still, just before I could "talk" to the alien again, to ask more questions, like if he was my age and gay, and if the rest of him looked as good as his face, said face slowly and sadly began to vanish, until Craig and I were again staring at each other in the mirror, and not into the eyes of dazzling blue.

"Damn," I said.

"Weird," Craig said.

"Again with the weird?"

He sighed and walked over to my bed, then sat down and looked my way. "Well, putting two and two together, the earthquakes seem to trigger the eyes, so at least we can assume that all this is somehow tied together. Now then, the alien said, or at least blinked, that he's in a separate universe from ours, but one in our same timeline. To me, that means that his universe was formed when ours was, but runs independently from our own."

"And the weird thing? I mean, apart from all of it?"

"The weird thing, or things, to be precise, is why now, and why here, and why you?" He held his hand up, thereby stopping me from affirming that, yes, it was all about me. I mean, the alien even looked like me. This was fate, kismet. I felt it. I had, as I said, always felt it, ever since the first quake I could remember. It was why I came home after college, too afraid to leave for good, to maybe miss something, something like all this. "Rhetorical, dude," he said. "I was asking the questions because I think I already know the answers, not because I care to hear you prattle on about your favorite subject, namely yourself."

I sat down next to him, skulking. "I don't prattle."

He grinned. "Uh-huh. Major prattling, dude. In any case, I think there are two universes, and they're all of a sudden meeting up, one world butting against the other, said butting causing the earthquakes. As to the mirror, somehow, we're able to see into their world and vice versa, but the door is only open for a brief period of time, as if the two universes bump, meet, and then separate."

I frowned. "So, they could separate and never come together again?"

He nodded. "They could meet one, twice, a few times, a few thousand times. It's impossible to tell. Though we have had the earthquakes for years now, so perhaps the two worlds are running side by side. Perhaps there's some kind of gravitational pull keeping them together, at least for the time being."

"But none of that explains why my mirror, why I feel this connection, why the owner of those eyes looks like me, albeit with eyes the color of brilliant sapphires."

He chuckled. "All I saw was blue."

"Figures."

"Anyway, as to why your mirror, why not? If there's a portal between the two worlds, your mirror is as good as any. As to the connection you're feeling, you probably just have a screw loose. And as to why he looks like you, well, maybe his screw is just as loose.

Or maybe they worship that Fabio guy in their universe." He stood. "Buy a wrench, dude. Tighten the screw. Save on those inevitable psychiatry bills."

I looked up at him. "You don't seem that shocked by all of this. I mean, we just talked, more or less, to an alien. We might be the first humans ever to do so."

He shrugged. "Guess I'm desensitized. Too many violent video games. Plus, I live with you. In other words, I'm already well-accustomed to alien encounters."

He was gone a moment later, leaving me alone with the mirror. I stared at it, but the connection was clearly broken, the tether severed. Still, I wasn't as nonchalant about the whole thing as Craig was. This was huge. No, nix that. THIS WAS HUGE! Yes, better. I mean, I met an alien. I talked to an alien. I popped a boner talking to an alien. Then again, I popped a boner when the wind blew, so that last thing was neither here nor there.

But what was I supposed to do now? Call the *Enquirer, TMZ?* In other words, cash in? Nah. No thanks. I'd been chosen. Chosen people didn't appear on the cover of *US. People,* maybe. *Rolling Stone* would've been nice. *OUT* for sure. Still, I shook my head. No, no, no. That's not what this was all about. Was it? Again, I shook my head as potential fame wrapped its sticky tentacles around me and threatened to drag me under.

In any case, I wanted to meet the alien, not scare him off—or worse: piss him off. I mean, what if he had a ray gun that could disintegrate me? *Ouch.* And no thanks.

And so, I'd have to wait, wait for another tremor, another encounter with Old Blue Eyes.

I hoped I wouldn't have to wait all that long.

FYI, I didn't.

§ § § §

It happened the next morning. I was in bed, wide awake. In truth, I'd barely slept. Instead, I tossed and turned, thinking about those eyes, wondering what the alien looked like beyond merely his stellar face. Or maybe make that interstellar. My mind buzzed at the possibilities. Why me? I wondered. Why here? And when would I see him again?

As to that last question, the when was in five seconds.

Five-four-three-two-one. Contact!

The bed began to bounce, my body along for the ride. My teeth chattered. My cock went *boing*. I hopped out of bed. Well, that is to say, I fell out of bed, tripping as the house shook one way and I the other. I then managed to crawl to the mirror, a smile instantly widening on my face.

"Morning," I said, the eyes, thank goodness, staring back at me. "What's up?" I stared down at my tenting jammies. "Apart from the usual."

The alien didn't answer. Um, okay, he might have, but without an auditory connection, I hadn't a clue. Still, he nodded and returned my smile in kind. I wondered where he was. Was he on a purple phosphorescent beach with a pink ocean lapping at his toes? Did he even have toes? For all I knew, he had flippers. Was he a merman? Was his mother named Ethel Merman?

But I digress. It happens. Frequently.

"Can you hear me?" Two blinks. *No? But he's answering me?* "Can you read my mind?" Two blinks. Then how were we sort of, kind of, communicating? It was then that I snapped my fingers. Because if he couldn't hear me, and he couldn't read my mind—a short read, by the way, and quite a dirty one—then that left only one option. "You're reading my lips." One blink, then a nod of his head, with a smile again spreading wide across his Harlequinny face. Such a beautiful smile. Such a beautiful man. But wait, was he a man or a boy?

"Can you blink your age." He blinked, and kept on blinking. He stopped at twenty-two. "That's my age!" So yes, a man, if just barely. My body trembled, even though the earth had already quieted down.

As before, all I could see was his handsome face. "What can you see of me? Just my face, all of me, the entire room?" He didn't reply. "Too many questions?" One blink. "Can you see my face?" One blink. "Anything more than that?" Two blinks.

Damn, this was frustrating. It would take forever to learn about him, about his world. And forever we didn't have. At most, we had minutes at a time. And what if our universes separated, if the connection forever broke? Then I'd never see him again. My heart ached at the thought. To come so close, only to be wrenched apart, was too much to bear. He was my future. I was certain of that. He was the one I'd been waiting for.

Drama queen much? Sure. So sue me.

I frowned, and said, "Is there another way for us to communicate? I mean, I'm sure lip reading is no more fun that blink-reading."

He seemed to laugh. I mean, that's what it looked like he was doing, but you never know with an alien. For all I knew, he was about to divide and split like an amoeba. Which was fine by me, as then there would be two gorgeous aliens to gaze longingly upon. In any case, he didn't divide or split, so he must've indeed been laughing. And nodding. Nodding, apparently, is universal. Or maybe make that multi-universal.

"So, we can communicate?" He nodded and blinked once, then opened his mouth and spoke. Not that I could hear him, but he was speaking, his mouth moving, lips parted, puckered, pursing. He was saying a word. "Commuter? There's a train from me to you?" No, that couldn't be it. Star Trek would've been awfully boring then, replacing the Enterprise with a choo-choo. *These are the voyages of the star train Lionel.* Yawn.

"Say it again," I told him. And so he said the word again, slowly, then again, and again. "Wait!" I shouted. "Computer! You're saying computer!" He nodded, the smile returning, vast as the Pacific.

I turned around and raced the few feet to my desk before flicking my laptop on, my breathing becoming heavy. I turned my wireless speakers on and waited, my heart pumping so fast it could give a jackrabbit a run for its money. And then, there it was…

"Greetings, Earthling." He laughed, the sound like seashells being tossed at the shoreline. It was a beautiful laugh, sublime.

I turned and looked at him in the mirror. "You're laughing."

He nodded. "Of course. What did it look like I was doing?"

I shrugged. "Dividing?"

He tilted his head. "Why would I divide? Sounds painful. Do humans do that? I thought you procreated to make more of you."

I fought to catch my breath. I was now talking to an alien, and one, at the time, in an entirely different universe. How was that possible? "How is this possible?"

"Which part?"

Good question. "Talking. How are we talking?"

He nodded. "I believe you call if Wi-Fi. I'm transmitting through a similar device. For all intents and purposes, our two worlds are connected at the moment, and so we can communicate wirelessly." His grin rose northward on his face. "Neat, huh?"

I shook my head. Not because it wasn't, as he said, *neat*, but because all this was too much to take in. I pulled up a chair, lest I should fall down—yet again, that is. I stared at him as he in turn stared at me. "What's your name?"

"You can call me Milo. That would be easiest for you. And you're Randy Rogers. And your brother is Craig. And you live in the city of San Francisco. And you like the band known as Britney Spears. And you're, what is called by your people, gay. And you just finished college."

"Wait, back it up," I said, holding my hand to the mirror.

"To which part? The Britney Spears thing? I listened to her." He frowned. "I, uh…I don't get it."

"She's a talented singer."

He shrugged. "If you say so."

"Anyway, how do you know all this? And how do you know I'm gay? Are your people monitoring me? Is there an anal probe in my future? A dissection? Will my lifeless corpse be used for educational purposes?" I pictured my body on a slab, a slab that was neither phosphorescent nor pink. I cringed.

Again, his head tilted. "Why would we dissect you? I can simply scan you for all necessary information. Dissection sounds far too messy. *Gross*, I believe you would say." His head righted. "Facebook."

"Huh?"

"Facebook. I learned about you on Facebook. We're Facebook friends."

I blinked in rapid succession. "Huh?"

"You already said that."

"Worth repeating." I turned and went back to my computer. I went to Facebook. I searched for a Milo. Shockingly, there he was. "Well, I'll be damned."

"Doesn't sound any better than dissected. Are you perhaps a masochist, Randy? It doesn't say so in your profile."

I had many hundreds of Facebook friends, most of whom I never met, nor would ever meet. Milo sent me a Facebook friend request. I accepted it based simply on how pretty he was. Call me shallow, but it's far easier to swim at that end of the pool.

"How?" I asked as I returned to my chair.

"Like I said, wireless. I have a device similar to your laptop, though far more advanced. When our worlds abutted, it became possible to communicate, though it took me a couple of days to learn your language. As for that communicating query, I chose Facebook. It seemed a popular medium."

"Wait," I said, ignoring the comment about learning English in two days. I mean, I'd taken Spanish for two years in high school, and I barely knew how to ask where the bathroom was. Anyway, back to that aforementioned *wait*. "So, your race is already communicating with mine? I'm not the only one?" I sighed. *Not the only one? Not special?*

"Nope, not communicating."

"But you just said that your people are communicating with us."

He shook his head. "No, I said it was possible to communicate; I didn't say we were communicating. What would be the point?"

"Lost me."

His shake turned to a nod. "Exactly."

I squinted his way. "Lost me further, Milo."

The nodding cranked up. "Lost. Your people would be lost, so to speak, if we communicated. It would be as if you tried to teach a puppy how to speak. Sure, a puppy is cute and all, but the lesson would ultimately be futile."

I think I got it. "Your people, like your computer, are too advanced for us?"

And still he nodded, his mane of blond hair bouncing all the while. "Too advanced, yes. Plus, your kind must learn for itself. You will thrive or perish at your own hands, just as my kind will do the same. Our laws are written as such. Observe, but do not interfere. Interference, in fact, like so much on my planet, would be illegal."

"So, your people are observing us?"

He shrugged. "Not so much."

"Huh?"

"Again with that word?" He exhaled exaggeratedly. "Anyway, you were interesting to watch, as a species, at first, but then it got old. It's like watching a television show. It might be good for a few years, maybe seven, eight, at most, but then you change the channel. Same with your kind. We have nothing to learn from you, scientifically, medically, or any other assorted *lys*."

"But here we are, you and me," I said. "We're communicating. You're no longer just observing. In fact, you've now changed my life, just by us talking, and so you are, in fact, interfering. Isn't that, like you said, breaking the law?"

He nodded. "Sure, but you're, you know, *cute*."

My head pounded. My dick did the same. Usually, it was the reverse, my dick in the lead. "So, you're gay, too?"

He shrugged. "This is a human construct. On my planet, we are all simply the same species. There are no divisions of race or gender or sexuality. We are all children of God."

My eyes went wide. "God? You believe in God? The same God as my God? The *in the beginning* God?"

"Same God, different beginning," he replied. "In the beginning, God belched. He created our universe. Yours was fourth in line. We got all the good stuff; you got the remainder. Since there was more of God in our belch, there were more of the basic building blocks, and so our universe evolved dramatically faster than yours, as did our species."

Yeah, that was a lot to take in. I mean, my family wasn't religious. God was like a distant uncle you saw once or twice a year. You loved him, sure, but in a hazy, peripheral fashion. In fact, you weren't even sure you were related to said uncle. Maybe by marriage. Maybe twice removed. Something along those lines.

"And you know all this how?"

He shrugged. "Legend. Lore. Mythos. How does one know anything when it comes to the supernatural?"

"And yet you believe?"

The shrug remained. Even that was adorable. Plus, it allowed me to see the faintest hint of shoulder. "It does explain my world and yours adequately enough. We do, after all, look the same, evolved similarly, have the same genetic makeup, more or less."

"Which is it?"

"Which is what?"

"More or less?"

"Ah," he ahhed. "Humans have forty-six chromosomes; my race has forty-seven."

"And what do you get with that added chromosome?" I pictured a second dick, three butt holes. For some reason, my pictures were always X-rated. I chalked it up to being barely an adult.

"Your race has the sex chromosomes X and Y; ours has evolved an additional Z, as yours most probably will in the future."

Oh my God, so he did have two dicks? Well, thankfully, I had more than one hole. Sadly, none of them were near enough to each other. Then again, maybe both his dicks were ginormously long.

"And what does this Z chromosome do?" I asked.

"It's mostly devoid of functional genes, similar to what our Y once was. Instead, it acts as a booster. We, as a race, are fairer than most, are smarter, even have a keener sense of humor."

I smiled. "So, it's a gay gene."

"That's a stereotype."

I shrugged. "You say tomato."

"Huh?"

I pointed at the mirror. "Ah, so you don't know everything."

He laughed. Again, my dick went *boing*. His laugh was Pavlovian that way. Pavlov threw his dog a bone; Milo threw me a boner. But back to the conversation. Or at least back a bit farther into it.

"You said I was cute," I said. "In fact, you and I look similar. Different eye and hair color, but similar. Is that why you contacted me?"

He started to reply, but sadly, just then, the connection shimmered and quivered and was promptly lost. I was now staring only at myself. My laptop speakers went silent. My dick, of course, remained stiff as a board. Yippee for that Y chromosome of mine!

Still, I wondered what it would be like to have that aforementioned Z.

Chapter 4

Days went by. There were no quakes, no signs of Milo. Suddenly, I knew what that expression about pins and needles was all about. And these were big-ass pins and massive needles, all jabbing relentlessly into my very soul—yes, see drama queen, as previously mentioned.

When we did finally have a quake, wouldn't you know it, I wasn't at home. I ran to the nearest bathroom and stared into the mirror, just in case, but even I knew it would be hopeless; the mirror back home was the conduit, the portal, *our* portal.

More days passed. I was bereft.

"What's wrong, dude?" Craig asked as he sat on my bed and played on his iPad. "You're, you know, *lackluster*. Like the gay's been sucked clean away."

"That's a visual."

He thought about it for a moment, then shuddered. "Sorry. My bad. Still, what's up?"

I shrugged as I stared forlornly at the mirror. "Milo." I'd already told my brother about the conversation. "I haven't seen him in nearly a week. What if the connection was lost? Like forever lost, I mean."

"Possibly, but we've been having these quakes for a little over twenty years. In the context of time and space, that's not even a blip. Best guess, the universes are still adjacent, the connection just temporarily severed." He looked up from his device. "Picture two quivering bubbles. They ebb and flow, side by side. Sometimes they touch; sometimes they don't. So long as they're on the same trajectory, they'll regularly touch down. Also best guess, they're at their closest at our point here in San Francisco and Milo's point on his planet, hence the earthquakes only occurring here."

"*Hence?* What happened to *ergo?*"

He shrugged and went back to his iPad. "Dropped it, dude. Didn't fit in with my new cooler persona."

I grinned. "Yeah, because *hence* is so friggin' cool. Like skinny jeans."

"I hate skinny jeans."

And I hated *hence*, but whatya gonna do? "Anyway, back to Milo. I hope he's okay. I have this, I don't know, this *feeling* that somethings wrong." I touched my chest. "It's that connection of mine, of ours, him and me. It's like there's a message coming through: danger, bad shit ahead. Step carefully."

He nodded and again looked my way. "I'm sure he's fine. You're just overreacting." He grinned and pushed his Bieber-like hair from his eyes. "You've been known to do that, you know."

I did, and I had, but not this time. "I'm sure you're right." Though I wasn't sure, not by a long shot. Plus, this is what happened not five seconds later...

As per before: five-four-three-two-one. Contact!

The earth rattled, first slowly and then with gusto. The bed bounced on the floor. My chair vibrated beneath me. I'd put a few quarters in a motel bed once. It sort of felt like that, only free this time, no spare change needed.

Craig looked at the mirror. I turned my speakers on and then gazed into those eyes, those eyes like sparkling pools of blue. Only, unlike before, the sparkle was gone, the smile as well. My belly tightened. I was right; something was wrong.

"Randy," he said in a whisper, or maybe the connection was off. Either way, something was most definitely wrong. "In trouble. They found out."

I gulped as Craig jumped up and stood by my side. "What's wrong?" Craig asked.

I turned to him, then back to the mirror. "Milo, this is my little brother, Craig." My gulp repeated, lemon-sized. Heck, it felt like an entire citrus orchard was stuck in my throat. "Who found out about what? And what kind of trouble?"

He glanced left, then right. His eyes were wide, nervous looking. He was breathing heavily. "The law. Not supposed to communicate. I thought it was safe. Had measures in place." He moved his face closer in. I did the same. "I was wrong, Randy. I shouldn't have contacted you. But…"

His face disappeared from view, though he was still connected, as was evident by the sound of the struggle that now filled my room and made my head swim. Michael Phelps should've swam so well, in fact.

"Milo!" I shouted. "Milo!"

The speakers went silent.

"Fuck," said Craig uncharacteristically.

I turned to him. "He's in trouble," I rasped. "It's…it's my fault." A tear welled up and spilled over, running down my cheek, my chin. I didn't know Milo, not really, but that connection of ours was so tangible that it felt as if someone had sucker-punched me in the gut.

"It's not your fault, dude. He found you. He contacted you. He knew he was breaking the law; he told you so himself."

"But why would he?" I asked. "Why me?"

Craig shrugged. "Don't know." Then he sighed. "And there's nothing we can do."

I dropped my head to my hands. *Nothing? Nothing at all?* "The mirror," I said. "It's a portal, right?"

"Of some sort. The worlds connect there, it seems. And?"

I turned and looked at him. "And I was hoping you could figure something out. You're the genius, after all." I pointed to myself. "Beauty." I pointed to him. "Brains."

He pointed to the mirror. "Solid." He pointed to me. "Idiot." He pointed to the door. "Leaving."

"Wait!" I shouted. "Please. Please don't go. I need your help. We need to help Milo."

He turned my way. "*We?*" I nodded, my eyes pleading. I gave good plea-eyes. He sighed, yet again. "Okay, I'll think about it."

"Not too long, though; they could be torturing him. Or worse."

He frowned. "Pressure much?"

I nodded. "Much, little bro. Much."

He left me alone in the deafening silence as my stomach gurgled and my heart felt like it could explode at any moment.

Yeah, yeah, drama queen. Didn't we cover that already?

§ § § §

More days went by, the hours ticking past as if they were coated in molasses. That is to say slowly, very slowly. Craig and I did very little interacting. When we were at home together, he was holed up in his room. He'd wisely learned from my mistakes, his door very much locked.

Mom and Dad were worried about me. I was worried about me. I was far more worried about Milo. Was he in jail? Was he being tortured, like I said? Sweat formed along my forehead as these thoughts formed and morphed into even worse thoughts.

An earthquake hit. I was home at the time. I rushed to the mirror, to the speakers, but there was nothing, no sign of Milo, no sound of him. My worry increased. I walked to Craig's room. I knocked on the door.

He unlocked it, opened it up, if only by an inch. "Almost."

My breathing was labored. "Almost? You mean, you think you can help him?"

He shrugged. "No clue. They don't teach inter-universe search-and-rescue in high school."

I sighed. "But you said *almost*."

"I did," he replied. "And maybe I have something. An idea,

anyway. Next earthquake, I'll be ready, okay?" He looked tired. He looked like Justin Bieber after a long night of shenanigans and cheesy tattooing.

"Okay, little bro. And thanks."

"Don't thank me yet, dude," he said as the door slowly shut and again locked. "Don't thank me yet."

§ § § §

It was two days later, two days of utter hell and frustration. It was late, close to midnight. I no longer slept. I was either awake or momentarily passed out. I was twenty-two and looking forty—a pretty forty, sure, but forty nonetheless. I was lying in bed, staring up at the ceiling. "Hang in there, Milo," I whispered. "We're coming for you."

The bed shook a second later. I hopped up and flicked on a light. Craig came barreling in a moment later, a large garbage bag flung over his shoulder. He closed the door behind him and tossed the bag to the pink carpet.

"What is all that?" I asked as he dumped the contents out.

He put his index finger to his lips. "*Shh*. Working."

I began to argue, which is how Craig and I did things, argumentatively, but then thought the better of it. Instead, I sat on the bed and watched him assemble the strange apparatus he'd invented. It took shape quickly enough. There was a basin on the floor, a structure of metal beams in the shape of a cube above that, a pan resting above that. There were some tubes running from top to bottom and back again. On the floor sat some sort of small motor. It looked like a...well, I hadn't a clue what it looked like. It looked like a mess of metal and tubes, like an erector set gone wrong.

"I have no idea what all this is," I freely admitted when it was at last complete.

He rose to hand me two emptied gallon jugs, now deplete of their milk. "Fill these."

"The cow went home for the evening."

He grimaced, eyes, as usual, rolling. "With water, jackass."

I nodded. "Water. Right. Be right back."

I raced to the bathroom. I raced as my mind raced. What was Craig up to? What was that apparatus he'd set up? And how would it help Milo? In any case, the jugs filled up quickly, and so back I rushed. I handed them to Craig. He filled the basin with the water, and then passed them back my way.

"Two more," he commanded.

I sighed. "Really?"

He mock-sighed me in return. "Did Einstein's assistants question his genius?"

"I doubt Einstein had assistants when he was eighteen, little bro."

He glared my way. "Don't doubt; fill."

Thus again commanded, I tore to the bathroom and filled up jugs three and four. By the time I'd done five and six, I was duly exhausted and even more frustrated. We didn't have that much time, after all. The portal never stayed open for more than ten minutes, and we were close to that already.

"Please tell me that was the last one," I said, now breathing hard.

"That was last one."

"Thank God," I exhaled as I watched him crouch down to the small motor.

"I'd say pray to him," he said, flicking the thing on. "Thank him after this is all over with."

The motor purred. Fortunately, it wasn't all that loud. Also fortunately, my parents slept on the first floor of our house, while Craig and I slept on the second. I mean, how would I have explained any of this, especially the waterfall Craig had suddenly flicked on in the middle of my bedroom.

"Pretty," I said. "But, uh, why does it suddenly look like the tropics in here?"

He rose and walked to the mirror. "Like I said a couple of days ago…" He touched the mirror. "Solid." He pointed to me. "Idiot." He pointed to the waterfall. "Leaving."

It took me a few seconds to put all the pieces together. "Wait," I said. "Water isn't a solid; it's a liquid."

"Eureka," he said with an exaggerated sigh.

"Now what?" I asked, instantly coming down off my high.

He slid my mirror out of the way and got down on the floor next to the waterfall. He'd put the basin on wheels, and so all the thing needed was a push before it was sitting where the mirror once had been.

"Now this," he said as he again stood next to me. "Go ahead."

I gulped. "Go ahead and, uh, what?"

He looked my way, his eyes burning like two tiny stars. I guessed that this is what Justin Bieber looked like just before he went on stage. "Try it out, dude," he said, then grabbed my hand and placed it in front of the downward flowing water.

"What if it works?" I asked. "What if it works and we're sucked into space? What if his world doesn't breathe oxygen? What if it works and we're trapped over there?"

He nodded thoughtfully. "All surprisingly good questions, dude. But there's one more: if we don't do this, what happens to Milo?"

I paused, but not all that long. In truth, I couldn't live with myself if I didn't know what happened to Milo. And no, that wasn't me being a drama queen, for a change; that was me knowing that I had a connection that had been severed, leaving me very much short-circuited, so to speak. Milo, I'd come to believe, was my destiny. Whether or not rightly so, it didn't matter; this is what I felt, and so that was all that mattered.

In other words, with just the slightest bit of trepidation, I stuck my hand through the water and promptly winced.

"What, what?" Craig asked, concern washing over his face. "Did it hurt? Is your hand disintegrating?"

I shook my head. "The water is cold."

He socked me one in the arm as he sharply exhaled. "Fucker." He then looked behind the waterfall. "Um, dude, just so you know, your hand isn't back there." He then locked eyes with me, those stars going all supernova-like. "Your hand, Randy, your hand is in another universe, boldly going where no hand has gone before."

My gulp repeated. I wiggled my fingers. They, in fact, still wiggled. Meaning, my hand hadn't, in fact, disintegrated. My hand was also not too cold or too hot, but, like the baby bear's porridge, just right. And so, I moved my arm further into the water, and further it did go. Which is why, since the body goes where the hand leads, I found myself walking through the waterfall a split-second later, saying through the spray, "Well, here goes nothing."

Though, of course, here went everything.

The very next moment, I was standing in an entirely different bedroom. I was wet. I was still in my jammies. And then, all of a sudden, Craig was standing next to me, also jammied and wet.

"Little bro," I said, "you followed."

"Yep," he said, eyes moving around the rather sparse room we found ourselves in, a room we were more than capable of breathing in. *Phew*. "Because pretty isn't going to rescue Milo; you need a bit of brains for this mission. Also, you're not exactly our people's best representative, so let me do all the talking, should it come to that."

"But you're only eighteen," I objected with.

He pointed my way. "And you're you." He shivered. "Maybe, all things considered, we should have brought a spare set of clothes." He turned to go back to our own bedroom, but the portal had already abruptly closed. "Oops. My bad."

I walked around the room. It looked something like a typical bedroom, though with some noticeable differences: for one, the bed hovered; the carpet was some weird fiber that both emanated warmth and felt like silky cotton beneath my feet; Milo's computer, or at least what he called a computer, or at least what I assumed was a computer, looked nothing like mine, the screen wide, maybe three feet, paper-thin, and just screen, no discernable electronics; oh, and the ceiling looked like the night sky, replete with actual twinkling stars and several moons glowing brightly above our heads. But that was it. No art. No pictures. No windows or doors. Nothing to indicate who or what lived there.

"Pretty," I made note, pointing upward. I looked over at my little brother, his face joyous as he stared into the sky above. Was it a real sky or simply an image of one? As to that, I hadn't a clue. "You scared, Craig?"

His neck went back to the starting position. He looked my way. "Scared, yep, but more excited than anything else. We're like Neil Armstrong, dude. Only, we took way more than one step for mankind here."

I smiled. He was right, and, truth be told, I too was excited. Scared shitless, but excited. Still, we had little time to revel in either. Milo, presumably, had been missing for days now. There was no sign of a struggle, but his bed was still made and it was nighttime, based on the ceiling visuals. Plus, his watch, or what looked like a watch, was on a nightstand. His wallet, or what looked like a wallet, was next to his watch. In other words, he either left quickly or was taken quickly. Either way, he wasn't there, nor had he made contact with me in all that time. When you put one and one together, you usually got two. I assumed the equation worked in this world as well.

Shaking myself out of my revelry, I noticed Craig was rummaging around in the nightstand, which was a smallish, metal, boxlike structure, the handles digitally represented, so that all you had to do was touch them and the drawers silently opened.

"Here," he said. "Put these on."

He handed me some slacks and a shirt, the material smooth, like silk, but with a feeling of durability. They were Milo's. I felt strangely weird taking them. Still, I was wet and in my jammies, which weren't exactly rescue clothes. So, I put them on, and, wouldn't you know it, they expanded to fit me like a T, as if they were tailored exactly to my measurements. A spare set of shoes and socks and undies all did the same miraculous trick. In other words, once we found an additional spare set of everything—which was basically the full extent of Milo's limited wardrobe—Craig, too, was in a form-fitting ensemble.

"Wow," he said, once we were both dry and dressed. "I'm guessing there aren't any seamstresses or tailors on this planet."

I grinned and plucked at my shirt. "Plus, this stuff must grow as you grow, so far less shopping needed." I smoothed out the silky fabric. "Too bad it's in green, though; not my favorite color. Blue would've been nicer." And yes, holy fuck, the shirt instantly turned blue. I pointed at the logo over my right pec. It was of a tree. Or maybe a bush. Heck, it could've been a hairy rock, for all I knew. "Shirt," I said, still grinning at Craig. "Change logo to the wording: rescue squad." Yep, bye-bye tree, hello requested lettering, stitched beautifully in gold.

"Dude," Craig said, wide-eyed. "I have a feeling that this world is gonna be full of surprises."

And it surely was.

Though the biggest surprise had nothing to do with the shirt on my back, or the wallet, which I'd taken, or the watch, which I'd slipped on my wrist, or the shoes on my feet, or the world waiting for us outside.

Nope, the biggest surprise was…well, come on, we're far too early in this story for that, aren't we?

Chapter 5

The wall parted at our approach. Craig and I left the bedroom, tiptoeing our way into a hallway. The house was silent, sparsely and coldly decorated, most of the furnishings familiar yet still different from what we were accustomed to. There was little color, no warmth to anything, no real signs of, you know, *life*.

Still, the tour needed to be a short one. If anyone was home, namely a parental unit, we thought it best that they didn't find us there in clothes that didn't belong to us, with a watch on my wrist and a wallet in my slacks that also didn't belong to us.

In other words, we were standing by a wall a moment later, desperately looking for a door. Thankfully, one slid open before I could even reach for a nonexistent knob. I jumped as it did this, and jumped even higher once we were confronted with the outside.

Okay, so I'll tell you what the outside looked like, but if all I'm going to do is explain the fantastical objects and sights we were soon to see, then this tale will quickly turn to nothing more than a travelogue of this strange and exciting world, whose name we still didn't know yet. In other words, a hat and a tree and a sidewalk and a car will henceforth be known as a hat and a tree and a sidewalk and a car, however, yes, fantastical they might be. If an added description is deemed necessary, don't worry, I'll provide it.

Fine?

So, here we go…

It was indeed nighttime. The sky looked just like the bedroom ceiling. It looked, in fact, like the sky on earth, except for the three moons instead of one, two of them larger and brighter than the distant crescent third, which glowed a beautiful orange.

I breathed in. The air smelled clean and fresh and cool. Craig breathed in with me. "Well, at least we didn't suffocate or inhale something poisonous," he said. "Points for that."

I nodded as I took in the neighborhood. It looked like the burbs, with houses separated by lawns of blue grass, the trees of various shapes and sizes, all of them well-pruned, most of them in flower. I heard what sounded like crickets, but could of course have been any manner of beast. It was all lovely, very otherworldly—which seemed apt, considering we were on another world, and all.

"Nice place," I said. "A bit cold-looking, a bit sterile, but nice."

He also nodded. "Let's take into consideration what you told me that Milo told you, that God belched this universe first and ours last. If such was the case—and that, of course, is a big if—then we can assume that the building blocks of both worlds were the same, that the atoms and molecules and elements formed similarly, that evolution took place in much the same way, that both worlds are somewhat similar, but with variation in color and shape and size. Still, similar just the same. Then take into account that, as Milo said, God gave them more *stuff* to work with, that they therefore evolved quicker. That would explain the advanced technology." He pulled at his shirt, which he'd changed from red to yellow. "Even these clothes are advanced. Still, for all intents and purposes, the people on this planet are human-like, presumably with human-like feelings and foibles."

"And?"

He shrugged. "Like you sad, it's all nice, familiar, so all we have to do is act normal and blend in."

"Should be easy enough."

He grinned. "If you were normal, then yes. In any case, don't be surprised by anything you see or hear or taste."

We began to walk down the sidewalk, though the sidewalk had us covered in that regard. Mainly because we didn't have to walk.

As soon as we stepped onto it, it began to move. No muss, no fuss.

"Hear, you said. But they won't speak our language, so hearing won't be of much use. Milo only spoke English because he studied it, so that he could communicate with me."

"Yep," Craig said. "I thought the same thing. Hand me your watch; I have an idea."

I took off the watch. I snapped it on Craig's wrist. That is to say, I touched it to his wrist and it snapped on itself, fitting like a, uh, glove. Craig spoke to the device. "How many languages are spoken on this planet?"

The watch lit up. It replied in English, "Eighty-seven." It didn't sound computery. In fact, it sounded, I don't know, sort of, well, *sexy*. Perhaps, I then reasoned, since these aliens had studied us over a period of years, English was recorded into their databases, that all things electronic, mechanical, could understand us and communicate with us, not just the watch.

In any case, Craig continued. "What is the name of this planet?"

"Planet Six. Planet Six is the sixth planet of twelve that revolve around the sun."

"How many are habitable?"

"Three. Planets Three, Four and Six all sustain life."

"Is there interplanetary travel?"

"The inhabitants of planets Four and Six travel between each other."

"Are they genetically similar?"

"They are identical. Planet Four was populated by Planet Six eighty thousand and twelve years ago. The two planets, however, speak numerous different languages and have different customs. The laws are similar. Relations are friendly."

"Enough," said Craig. "Off."

He turned to me. "Well, that was interesting," he said. "So, if we get caught, we can say we're from Planet Four, which might explain why no one has a record of us. And if someone tries to communicate with us, pretend to be mute and let the watch answer for us. Fingers crossed that none of this sets off any bells or whistles."

"Or nuclear bombs or death rays."

He winced. "Yeah, or those." He again looked down at the watch and spoke. "Will you be able to cover for us if questioned?" he asked. "Do you understand the request?"

The watch replied, "I will, and I do. No problem. I have covered for my owner numerous times before."

I wondered for what. I wished we had time to find out. Sadly, time is something we did not have.

We continued on our way, the sidewalk meandering us through the neighborhood at a fairly good clip. In the distance, brighter lights could be seen. This, I figured, was a city. From there, we could probably access the rest of the planet. From there, we could hopefully get to Milo. Except, of course, we hadn't a clue where Milo was—or if Milo himself still, uh, *was*.

I turned to look at my brother. "Well, this is great and all, but it's not getting us anywhere."

"I guess we could simply ask the watch where he is."

"That easy?"

He shrugged. "Seems to me, everything about this planet is about making things easy. I suppose that's the purpose of technology, how it evolves over time. With each generation, things just get easier and easier."

"Okay, so ask it."

Craig paused. "What if…what if we don't like the answer?"

My heart pounded, belly gurgling at the inference. "Then we go home, right?" Again, fingers crossed. I mean, Planet Six was a nice place to visit, but I wouldn't want to live there. I mean, blue grass and purple leaves? No thanks. Green is just fine for me. Plus, I like clothes shopping. I find it quite Zen. Seems like by making it so easy on Planet Six, they took out all the fun. And yes, I was procrastinating here, postponing answering Craig, terrified at what we might find—or might not find, namely Milo.

"Hello," said Craig, thereby shaking me out of my reverie. "Earth to Randy."

I forced a smile. "That phrase seems to take on a whole new meaning here, little bro."

He nodded. "Is it weird to feel homesick after just fifteen minutes?"

I'd been feeling the same. "Nope." I pointed at the watch, a gulp riding like a runaway elevator along my throat. "Ask. Quickly. Like ripping off a Band-Aid."

He lifted his wrist to his mouth. "Where is the owner of this device, the person familiarly known as Milo."

"Current exact whereabouts unknown," came the reply. Actually, the watch sounded like a coffee commercial. A sexy coffee commercial, but still. *Good to the last drop.*

"Last known whereabouts?"

"Body GPS was last recorded in City Northeast Nineteen, two days ago."

Fear suddenly gripped me. "Two days ago, his body GPS got turned off. Does that mean he's…does it mean…that he's *dead?*" The last word came out part whisper, part sob, all misery.

"No," replied the watch. "Body GPS would still register in death, unless the body was incinerated." I clutched my chest. It felt as if I'd been stabbed there. "Other options for body GPS cessation: intentional blockage of signal by outside source; device malfunction; encasement in thick enough material so that signal cannot transmit properly."

Craig nodded. "And the probability of malfunction?"

To which the watch replied, "Point-two percent."

"Off," said Craig, and the watch went black. "So, that leaves death or intentional signal blockage or possible imprisonment. In any case, at least we know where to start looking for him."

"City Northeast Nineteen," I said, and the sidewalk abruptly stopped, which meant that, as suspected, all mechanical devices on this planet, or, at the very least, the people movers and a lone sexy-talking watch and a few articles of clothing, understood English.

"Huh," Craig said. "Seems this sidewalk doesn't go that way."

"Think they have Uber on Planet Six?"

Craig shrugged. "Probably something similar." He again talked to the watch. "What is the easiest way to City Northeast Nineteen?"

"City Northeast Nineteen is approximately seven Earth miles from your present location. Underground transport will take you four minutes. Mover at southwest corner will have you at the terminal in sixteen minutes. Board at station four, heading north. Cost in Earth currency is three dollars and forty cents."

I looked at Craig. "We don't have any currency."

"Hand me Milo's wallet."

Milo's wallet was a thin metal case with several cards inside. I assumed these were some sort of credit cards or card keys, and, to quote Craig, *ergo*, that it really was some sort of wallet. In any case, I handed it over to Craig.

"Is there a payment method held within this?"

The watch emitted some sort of scanning light. The wallet, for its part, seemed to activate upon being scanned. An image of Milo appeared on the cover. It was some sort of photo ID, it seemed. My heart pulsed at the sight. A second later, my dick did the same.

"Payment method within," replied the watch.

"How do we pay for underground transport?" Craig then asked.

"Underground transport will scan case. Payment will be made upon scan."

Craig looked at me. "Not a good idea."

"Why is that?" I asked. "Sounds easy enough. Just like the subway back home, more or less."

He shook his head. "They scan the wallet, someone somewhere will know that Milo is travelling. What if bad people find this out?

What if bad people are monitoring for such an occurrence? What if bad people already know that Milo can't possibly be travelling?"

I sighed and put my mouth near the watch, which was as strange as it sounds. "Is there another way to pay for underground transport, other than by scan? A currency of some sort?"

"Currency on Planet Six was made inactive two hundred and ninety-four Earth years ago."

I sighed and looked at the watch. If it was going to be our, you know, *friend*, I'd have to call it something. "Do you have a name?"

"Milo refers to me as Tag Heuer."

I laughed. I laughed because it was better than crying. I laughed because clearly Milo had a sense of humor—and, of course, great taste in men, namely moi. "Okay, Tag, is there another way to get into the underground transport that doesn't involve getting scanned."

"Only other way is illegal."

I nodded. "Still, is there a way?"

It paused, however briefly. I assumed it was thinking, so to speak. "Workers are not scanned for payment."

Craig raised his hand to ask a question, old habits dying hard. I hope we didn't meet the same fate—the dying part, that is. Hard or easy. "Um, but we're not workers."

"You asked a question," Tag replied. "This is your answer. You could also walk to your destination. It would take approximately six Earth hours."

Craig looked at me. I looked at him. "We'll work it out when we get to the terminal," he said.

I nodded as we made our way to the southwest corner of the block. We hopped on the sidewalk. *Whoosh*, we were underway. "Underground transport," I said. The sidewalk kept moving, so we must've been headed in the right direction.

We passed houses, as before, but they began to thin out, replaced by small buildings, all made of various metals. There was no wood, no brick. Everything gleamed in the moonlight—or, as was the case, moonslight. I gazed up and around and over and down. All was new to me, but with a feeling of familiarity. A wall was a wall, a lawn a lawn, as if the evolution of both species tended toward a certain commonality.

Sixteen minutes later, and just as Tag had promised, we spotted the terminal. Well, it looked like a terminal, given that it was well-lit and wasn't like the other nearby buildings. Plus, it had steps going down into the ground. But hey, it could've been a post office for all we knew, or even a police station. "Please don't let this be a police station," I whispered as we made our way in and down, and down, and down some more, the steps, thank goodness, becoming yet another people mover. As for them—the people, that is—it was late, as was evident by the sky and the moons high above, so, as yet, we hadn't seen any. For that, I was both grateful and disappointed. I mean, did everyone look like Milo on this planet? Stunning, I mean? Like me, I mean?

Then, at last, we were in a vast underground cavern. It was reminiscent of the photos I'd seen of Grand Central Station, with tunnels trailing off from the outer walls. But where the station in New York was all brick and stone and cement, this was again metal, sheets of it in various metallic hues, all lit by recessed lighting. It was both beautiful and stark. In fact, as I thought about it, that expressed everything we'd seen thus far: beautifully stark, no adornments, simplistic.

We walked to one of the tunnels. There were sensors around the rim: a thin strip of metal with moving green lights—and sensors, we knew, were not our friend.

"There has to be someone working here, some station agent, a janitor," I said. "Tag told us that the workers don't get scanned for payment, so there has to be workers, right? But where? I don't see anything, no ticket booth, no janitor's closet, no security, nothing."

Craig nodded and turned around, and around, and around again. "Nope, nothing." He scratched at his chin and squinted his eyes. "They have to pee, don't they?" He lifted his wrist. "Tag, where is the closest bathroom?"

"You must request it."

"The bathroom?"

"Yes."

Craig shrugged and said, "Bathroom," his voice echoing in the vast, empty space around us.

And just like that, the wall closest to us split, a room inside revealed, brightly lit.

"This stark look is on purpose," said Craig. "They seem to like things to look bare, plain. Everything has a function, but you have to ask for it, otherwise, it's kept out of sight." He moved to the bathroom. "Be right back. Need to test an idea."

"It's a bathroom," I said as he walked inside. "What's to test? You pee and poop in there." Right? They did that on Planet Six, didn't they? Or did Tag take care of that as well? If and when I ever made it back to Earth, I'd have to invest in the watch industry. You know, once I had two nickels to rub together.

Craig returned. "Nice bathroom."

"Stark, I bet."

He nodded. "Very." He held up a piece of what looked to be tissue paper. "This is my idea."

I grinned. "Are we going to festoon their trees. I bet these people prefer treats over tricks, little bro."

He shook his head. "Just watch."

I watched as he dropped the tissue paper. It fluttered slowly to the also metal ground. In a flash, a robotic device appeared from inside the wall. The tissue paper didn't know what hit it. One minute it was minding its own business, the next, *slurp*, it was gone, as was the robot.

"Fascinating," I said as I patted Craig's back. "Who needs TV when you have that?"

He pushed my arm away, eyes summarily rolling. "No, you idiot. My idea was that there are no ticket agents, no janitors, no security guards, because everything, absolutely everything, is automated."

"But Tag said there are workers."

He nodded. "The first tissue was part one of the test." Another tissue appeared, this one also dropped, also fluttering to the floor, the robot again appearing. Only, this time, when it slurped, we, or at least Craig, was a not so innocent bystander. That is to say, the robot slurped and Craig kicked, the robot tipping over, filling the otherwise noiseless cavern with a slight buzzing sound.

"Now what?" I asked.

"Bathroom!" he shouted. "Run!"

The bathroom again parted open and in we ran. The doors, or whatever they were, slid closed behind us. When I turned, expecting to see metal, I could, in fact, see the station beyond. "Cool." I had a feeling that the houses did the same thing. It was dark when we were in Milo's home and when we were riding the sidewalk. I hadn't noticed windows before. Now, I gathered there simply weren't any.

He shushed me. "Watch."

I watched. A minute or so later, a man appeared in a grey jumpsuit. He looked around, apparently confused that there was a robot on its side and no people in sight. In any case, he righted it and the robot went back to whence it came. The man then walked to the wall and also disappeared from whence he came.

Craig looked at me. "People, or at least people in this station, only work to repair anything that is automated, which, it seems, is everything. I bet, if we go through that same wall he just went through, we'd eventually come out onto the transport platform."

"If we can go through the same wall," I said. "But how? The wall had to have scanned him before he went through. Your average person can't get in there, I'm betting."

He smiled brightly. "Good thing I'm not average then."

In fact, I was thinking the same thing. I gave my brother a lot of shit—seriously, a lot—but I certainly appreciated his genius, especially now. And as for that aforementioned now, we were now headed back to the bathroom.

"Tag," he said, once inside.

"Yes, sir?"

"Craig. Please, call me Craig."

"Yes, Craig?"

"Do you have some sort of weapon, a protection device. On Earth, we would have what we call Mace."

"All arms, weapons, ammunitions, are illegal, Craig. I searched this *Mace* of yours. I am not equipped to spray."

"Uh-huh," he said. "But if you were used to protect, or at least momentarily immobilize, even if illegally, are you equipped?"

"Yes, Craig," Tag replied. "Who would I immobilize?"

"There are workers here in grey uniforms."

"Government employees, Craig. Even more illegal. Long confinement if caught. Possibly worse."

Craig nodded. "So, we won't get caught."

To which, sadly, at least for us, Tag informed, "Probability of getting caught ranges from seventy-four to ninety-three percent."

"What is the probability of an Earthling standing in a bathroom on Planet Six."

"Infinitesimally small, Craig."

Craig rubbed his hands together as his smile reappeared. "Yeah, there you go then." He then turned to me and said, "Now all we need is a distraction, something to get that jumpsuited dude in here."

We were in a bathroom. There were stalls. That was all. I walked into one of them. There was a bowl below and a bowl above, tissue paper off to the side. I assumed the bowl below was a toilet, the one above a sink. These people hadn't invented the bidet, yet, or perhaps simply didn't enjoy the technology. A wet asshole is not to everyone's liking, after all. "Clog the toilet bowl," I suggested.

He snapped his fingers. "Good idea." He scooped up a massive roll of paper and stuffed it into the lower bowl. He looked around for a way to flush it, but there was none, and so, "Flush," he said. Only, the bowl didn't flush. Instead, the bowl lit up and the paper instantly evaporated. *Poof!*

"Cool," I said, once again.

"Not cool, dude," Craig said. "*That* was our diversion."

"Oh yeah. Right." I looked around. I stuck my hand in the bowl above, hoping I could somehow clog or break that instead. "Wash." And no, water did not shoot out. Again, the bowl lit up. I assumed I'd just been disinfected and deodorized. Perhaps irradiated. I hoped for the former. "Damn," I said, then added, "Tag, how is the door of this stall held on?"

Tag scanned the stall. "Magnetically, sir."

"Randy."

"Dictionary defines as impassioned, lustful, horny."

I blushed. At a watch. Weird, but true. "Randy. It's my name, Tag." And frequently occurring adjective.

"Magnetically, Randy."

I nodded. "Can you demagnetize it so that the door comes off?"

"Yes, Randy. Please move outside the stall and hold me up to the hinges."

Which is just what we did, the door falling off in a loud clang a moment later. We then turned and stared through the wall behind us, the man in grey quickly appearing before heading our way.

"Hide," Craig said.

Fortunately, there were stalls on either side, and so hide we did, just as the jumpsuited man walked inside.

He cursed, I think. Hard to tell, since he was speaking Planet-Sixian, but it sounded like a curse. Something, I imagined, along the lines of: *what the fuck?*

I crouched down. The stall door had a few inches of space between it and the floor. I stared at the man's legs. I stared beyond at Craig, who was smiling and waving at me. I waved back. I pointed up. The man in grey was lifting the door from the floor.

Now, I mouthed.

Craig held his wrist out of the stall and whispered, "Immobilize government employee, Tag."

Said government employee said something, something that again sounded like: *what the fuck?* Then he screamed and dropped the heavy door onto his foot. That is to say, he screamed and dropped once Tag shot out some sort of bright beam of light, which must've temporarily blinded the government employee, causing him to, you know, scream and drop.

That was our cue. We jumped out. The man was on the floor, one hand rubbing his foot, the other his eyes. He had a card attached to his jumpsuit. I grabbed it. Craig said, "Sorry, dude."

"Yeah," I said. "Sorry."

To which the man said, yet again, or so I'm assuming, something like *what the fuck?*

We were running across the cavernous station a moment later. "Open!" I shouted, holding up the card we'd stolen.

The hidden doors slid open. We, in turn, slid inside. I was huffing. Craig was puffing. I turned. I could see through the wall and beyond. The government employee had yet to give chase. I again turned around. We were in an antechamber of sorts. There were jumpsuits hanging from the wall.

"Put them on," I said. "Then at least we can blend in, in case we run into anyone back here."

He nodded. "Good idea."

"Really?" I said, then smiled.

He shrugged. "Too bad it took hopping between universes for it to happen."

My smile promptly flatlined.

We were dressed a few seconds later, the uniforms, like the clothes beneath them, shrinking and/or growing to fit our bodies. I held the card we'd purloined up to the material. It somehow locked onto it.

We turned, we ran out of the room and down a hall. There were no rooms, no doors, no end, but there were signs here and there, signs in a language we couldn't, of course, translate. Well, not me and Craig, anyway.

"Tag," Craig said. "Where is the entryway to the station platform that will take us to City Northeast Nineteen."

Sadly, for us that is, before Tag could reply, a very loud alarm sounded, echoing down the hallway.

I looked at Craig, eyes wide. Craig looked at me, eyes wide.

"Fuck," we both said in unison.

To which Tag added, "Probability of getting caught is now ninety-eight percent."

"Shut up, Tag!" I shouted. "Shut the fuck up!"

Chapter 6

We jumped through the first entryway on our right. Amazingly, we jumped correctly. That is to say, we were on the platform we needed to be on. Two minutes later, we were on a train headed to City Northeast Nineteen. Actually, we were sitting in a massive metal box, on a seat, with hundreds of other seats on either side, staring through the metal to the landscape beyond. There was another row behind us that faced the opposite way. The seating condition was unnerving, as we were speeding at an impossibly fast rate while staring through the metal, which made it seem like there was no metal there to begin with, so that it felt more like a rollercoaster ride than public transportation.

It was late. We were alone on the train. "To recap," said Craig, turning my way, "we've been on this planet less than an hour; we've mugged a government employee; stolen government-issued jumpsuits; have a veritable stranger's credentials on us, namely Milo, who has probably been kidnapped; we're on the lamb from the law; and our only friend in the entire universe—a universe not our own, for that matter—is a watch named Tag Heuer."

I nodded as I ticked each item off on my fingers. "Yep, seems about right," I replied with a grin. "But at least we're headed in the right direction."

"Presumably."

I touched my hand to my chest. "I feel it, still. I feel *him*. I can't explain it, Craig, but that connection of mine, of his and mine, is real." I smiled, despite that fearful recap of his. "Trust me, we're headed his way."

He shrugged. "If you say so, dude."

"That word not getting old yet?"

His shrug shrugged higher. "Nope. Not yet."

Four minutes later, as Tag had foretold, we pulled into City Northeast Nineteen.

The doors, or whatever they were, slid open, and out we stepped into another station, an even larger one than before. And yet, once again, we were utterly alone.

"Strange," said Craig.

"Yeah. I mean, I know it must be late, but how can we be the only people travelling? How can that one guy we mugged be the only person we've seen."

His shrug reappeared. "Like I said, strange."

We exited the station, emerging into a city illuminated by the lunar trio.

Our heads craned up. And up. And up even more.

"Holy cow," Craig uttered.

"Um, yeah."

Picture New York. Now picture the buildings of New York made completely out of glimmering metal, no windows, no doors. Now picture the buildings of New York twice as high. Got it? Yes? Okay, now also picture New York with no cabs, no noise, no people, and, lastly, no pigeons.

Eerie, yes? And, you guessed it, beautifully stark. This was like a coloring book version of a city: all outline, nothing filled in.

Craig pointed up. "They don't need windows; you can see through the metal from the inside, obviously. And the doors are hidden. You walk up; they slide open."

"But where are all the people who either live or work in these buildings?"

"Maybe everyone sleeps at night. Maybe everyone works nine-to-five jobs? Maybe they have a curfew on this planet, or at least in this part of it. Maybe it's dangerous to be out at night?"

I managed a smiled as I pointed at the both of us. "Muggers."

He also smiled. "Exactly."

"In any case, we're here, and so now what?"

"Tag," said Craig, his wrist held up. "Where was the last location Milo was known to be at?"

"Milo was last recorded at approximately one Earth mile from here. City Northeast Nineteen is the fourth largest city in this quadrant, Craig. Perhaps, it would be easier if you let me lead the way."

Craig nodded eagerly. "Yes, please, Tag. Also, Tag, where are all the people?"

"I don't understand, Craig."

"The people. Why are we the only people outside at this time?"

"I still don't understand, Craig. There are other people outside at this time."

"In this city?" I asked.

"Yes," replied Tag as his scanner illuminated the space around us. "In a four Earth-mile radius, which is the limit of my scanner's range, there are six people outside."

"Not including the two of us?" I said.

"Correction then, Randy," said Tag. "There are four people outside at this time, not including the two of you."

I blinked. I blinked again. That didn't make any sense. "In an entire four-mile radius?"

To which Craig added, "How many total inhabitants live in City Northeast Nineteen, Tag?"

"As of the last census, Craig, City Northeast Nineteen was the home to eight-hundred."

Again, I blinked. Again, I blinked again. "Eight-hundred-thousand or eight-hundred-million?"

"No," said Tag. "Eight-hundred."

"In the fourth largest city in this quadrant?" I said, staring up at all the mammoth buildings, which stretched out in every direction as far as the eye could see. "What, does each person get their own skyscraper?"

But before Tag could answer, we heard, "There they are!" Well, it sounded something like that, anyway.

I turned and spotted three men, all of them in grey. Jumpsuits were apparently very popular on Planet Six. Craig and I looked at each other for a brief, terrifying moment before we took off running. I'd like to say we ran into the night, into the shadows, but Planet Six had three bright moons and reflective metal buildings. In other words, good luck finding a dark corner to hide in. I mean, the place was like Disney during the Fourth of July. Bright, I'm saying. A Klieg light should be so bright. Which is why we decided to simply run around corners, around buildings, to try and lose them in the maze that was this weirdly empty, massive city.

Craig suddenly stopped, both of us very nearly out of breath and very fully terrified. "I have an idea. Longshot, but we're desperate."

"Works for me."

He nodded. "Okay, wait here."

"Alone?" My mouth was so dry that it made the Mojave seem like the Mississippi in comparison.

He pointed to the nearest building. "I'm just going over there. Stay put."

Again, I nodded and then watched as he ran to where the front door would be—had any of these buildings had front doors. He lifted his arms. "Open," he said, and waved his hands. Nothing happened. The buildings, or at least this one, must've been locked. He ran back to me. "Now, you try."

"You want me to give the building jazz hands?"

"Humor me, dude?"

I shrugged. It beat running like a chicken in a hen house. And so, I walked up to the building, flung my arms around, and said, "Open."

Voila, the wall slid apart, revealing the inside. Thank the Lord.

Craig pushed me inside. I tripped and fell from the inertia. He tripped over me. The wall closed behind us. We were now both sprawled on the hard floor, but at least we were safe. He then pointed at the wall we'd fallen through. My heart literally stopped when we saw the three men who had been chasing us. They were milling around outside, looking everywhere for us. Craig put his index finger to his lips. Silence permeated the dark space around us, save for our breathing and my heart pounding in my ears.

A minute went by, two. It felt like hours. Still, eventually they disappeared from sight.

"Tag," Craig whispered, "does a government employee card get you into the buildings?"

"Affirmative, Craig," Tag replied. "Government employees have full access to all non-security buildings."

"Why is that?" I asked.

"Multiple roles," said Tag. "Government employees are similar to Earth police, Earth janitors, Earth mechanics. They require access. It is vital."

I turned to Craig. The space around us was dark save for the meager light that worked its way to us from the outside. "I don't get it. Why would a government employee need to have all three job duties, and three that have seemingly nothing in common?"

Craig yawned, causing me to yawn in return. "Too tired to think, dude," he said. "Been a long night." He looked down at the watch. "Does this building have any beds, Tag?"

"Floors five through ninety, Craig."

"Can you find us an empty apartment to crash in?"

"Floors five through ninety are vacant, Craig."

Craig shrugged. I shrugged. We were exhausted. We were confused. Par for the course since we'd arrived. And so, we found the equivalent of an elevator and went to the fifth floor. There were no doors, just small plaques on the metal wall. By now, we knew the deal, and so with my ID card, I opened up two side-by-side entryways.

"I'll come get you at daybreak, little bro. Maybe then, some of this will make sense. Better still, maybe we'll be closer to finding Milo." I started to turn, to go to find a bed, when I asked, "Can I have Tag?"

He nodded and handed the watch over. "Have him wake us in five hours. That should be enough sleep, and not too much time not spent finding Milo. Plus, hopefully, that will put five hours of distance between us and those guys in grey."

I hugged him. I never hugged Craig. Now seemed as good a time as any.

"Weirdo," he said, hugging me back.

"Nerd," I said, and then turned and entered through the adjacent door, both doors closing in sync behind us. And yes, there really were no doors, but the correct wording, like most everything on the planet, escaped me.

The lights came on as soon as I entered. Not surprisingly, the apartment was, you guessed it, stark. In fact, it was empty.

"Bed," I said.

A bed slid out from a wall. It was already made with a blanket and sheets and a pillow, of sorts. I had a feeling that if I asked for a sink or a shower or a stove, those too would appear. But I didn't want any of those; I just wanted to lie down. And so I de-jumpsuited and de-clothed before hopping in. The sheets were smooth and silky and surprisingly warm, considering their thinness.

"Tag," I said.

"Yes, Randy?"

I looked down at the watch. "You got any selfies of Milo?"

Tag didn't answer, and no, a picture of Milo didn't appear on Tag's surface, nor did one project on the wall by my side. Instead, a

3-D image hovered just above me, Milo in profile, real as life, if not oddly illuminated.

"Whoa," I said, the image so clear that I could see the pores on his face, every strand of glorious blond hair, even the sparkle in his eye. "So handsome."

"He says the same of you, Randy."

I smiled. "He does? He talks to you about such things?"

"I am Milo's friend."

I squinted my eyes. *Really? A friend? The watch?* I shook my head. *Such an odd planet.* And then I thought of a new strange request for said friend. "Do you have an emoji, Tag, a representation of some sort of yourself?"

Again, Tag didn't answer or show me an image. Mainly because Tag was suddenly standing by my side, tall and slender, handsome as, well, as Milo himself, with blue hair and porcelain skin, a surprisingly bright smile on his face, which was warm and inviting. He, like the face still hovering above me, was lit, a sort of halo surrounding his entire form. Like his voice, Tag was, I'll admit it, sexy. Sexy as all hell. Hell and heaven, actually. Throw in Purgatory, to boot.

"Whoa," I repeated. "You're hot."

"I feel no such sensation, Randy," he replied, mouth moving, eyes blinking.

"Handsome. You're handsome."

"A subjective word," he said. "I have many thousands of form variations. I was, in fact, designed by Milo. I can also be a woman." Tag was suddenly a woman. "I can be a small boy." Yep, Tag was suddenly a small boy. "I can be a faithful pet." And no, Tag wasn't a dog so much as something resembling a squishy octokitty. It didn't look like something you wanted to play with so much as shoo away.

"Back to Milo's preference, please, Tag." Tag reappeared. "Naked." Tag's clothes vanished, leaving a stunningly naked man by my side, smooth as the sheets above me, though not tenting as those now were. "Milo designed this as well?" Tag nodded, while I instinctively reached out to grab his dangling willy. Sadly, my hand went right on through. It glowed from within the image, which felt both odd and unsettling.

"Do you have a full body selfie of Milo?"

Milo was suddenly standing next to Tag. He was dressed in similar clothes to what we'd borrowed from him. He was shorter than Tag, perhaps a little less than six feet, about my height, about my medium build, nicely defined. My heart pittered and then promptly pattered at the sight of him, this being the first time I'd seen him below the neck.

"This is a photo taken and reproduced as a 3-D image?"

"Photo? No, Randy. We have no such thing on this planet. I simply had to scan Milo. I can now put Milo in any position, standing in front of any backdrop, doing any sort of activity, just as I can stand in any position, in front of any backdrop, doing any sort of activity. It is simple technology."

"Uh-huh," I said. "Simple."

I pushed myself up onto my elbows and lowered the sheets. I was naked. I was so hard that a crowbar would bow in reverence. "Both of you naked, please, Tag, with Milo fucking you."

Presto! Milo was ramming his prick up Tag's ass, real as day, even with grunts and groans and sweat glistening across his slightly hairy chest. I jumped out of bed, cock swaying, creating a minor breeze in its wake. FYI, I was no longer exhausted. No less confused, sure, but now fully caffeinated, so to speak.

I walked around the holographic spectacle, taking in every inch of Milo, head to toe, every hair, every freckle, all of it perfectly reconstructed.

"You don't mind this, Tag?"

"Mind what, Randy?"

"Me having your friend do this to you?"

Tag looked up at me, blue hair hanging over his forehead. Tag had emerald eyes that locked onto mine like a vise. "It is not real, Randy. Milo cannot fuck, as you put it, me. I cannot feel this fucking.

The image is simply constructed for your viewing pleasure. Are you not pleased?"

I grabbed my cock. It and me were both pleased. Which was as gross an understatement as ever there was one.

"Pleased, yes," I said. "Stop fucking. Have Milo stand before me, naked, erect, hands at his sides."

In an instant, Tag was standing beside Milo, both of them naked, erect, hands by their sides. I gulped at the sight. I'd, of course, seen porn on my computer before, but that was nothing compared to this. That was like comparing an old black and white TV to an IMAX screen.

"Does Milo put me in such positions?"

Tag nodded. "Sort of, Randy. Seeing as I couldn't previously scan you, I had to extrapolate from Facebook. Still, Milo seemed satisfied with the result."

"Scan me now, Tag." A beam shot out from the watch. It took all of a split-second. "Place me in between the two of you."

I jumped as a duplicate me appeared between them, just as naked, just as erect. It was me down to the freckle above my nipple, down to the hairs that trailed beneath my bellybutton, to the one ball that was slightly heavier than its neighbor, to the crooked big toe.

"Handsome," I said, mainly because Tag wouldn't call me out on it like my brother would've.

"If you say so, Randy."

I nodded. "Have me kiss Milo."

Of all the things I could've had us do, of every position we could've suddenly been in, this was all I wanted to see, all I so desperately wanted to do. Well, okay, fine, not *all*, but firstly.

And so, I watched intently as Milo and I were in a tight embrace, kissing passionately, his hands in my hair, mine running down his lower back. As I jacked my cock, balls bouncing against the silky sheets, and as I almost immediately came and came and came some more, I prayed: *Please let this happen for real, God. Please let Milo still be alive, so that this can happen for real.*

§ § § §

Tag woke me up exactly five hours later. He was still a shiny, naked hologram. It was a pleasant if not wholly strange way to greet the day, and greet a flaccid dick not five inches from my face—and one that had a blue bush to match the hairs on his head. In other words, the carpet matched the drapes. Go figure.

"Good morning, Randy."

I grinned. "Can you wake up Craig like that?"

He shook his head. "I cannot go that far from the device on your wrist, at least not through a wall or around several corners."

"Pity." I looked around. I needed a shower, seeing as I was still sticky from, well, *you know*. I didn't see a shower. I needed to pee. There was no toilet. I needed to eat something. There was no kitchen, no stove, no food. Still, I knew all I had to do was ask.

And so:

"Shower."

There was no shower. Instead, from the ceiling lowered a tube. As with the bowl in the station bathroom, a light bathed over me. I didn't feel anything but a slight bit of warmth, and yet, I did feel completely clean about five seconds later.

"Novel," I said.

"You care for a book, Randy? What topic?"

I shook my head. "Novel. Original. Fresh. Innovative."

Tag nodded. Tag was still naked. I liked Tag naked, in that Tag looked quite beautiful naked. Milo had designed him well. Kudos to Milo. Lucky for me.

"Pee," I then said.

A bowl emerged through a slit in a nearby wall. I peed. The pee was evaporated away almost instantly, a faint aroma of something akin to jasmine wafting up to meet my nostrils.

"Blow nose," I said.

Out popped a tray with a bowl of tissues, ones similar to those in the train station bathroom. I blew, the sound echoing around the nearly empty space around me.

"Breakfast."

A tray emerged from the opposite wall, a bowl perched atop, something akin to, well, paste within. The paste didn't smell like jasmine. The paste didn't smell like anything. The paste was simply paste, nearly as grey as the jumpsuit I'd recently been wearing.

"What is it?" I asked.

"Nutrition," said Tag.

"Yes, but what kind?"

He tilted his head. "I do not understand. You eat. Your body utilizes the nutrients. The food is standardized to meet your needs, based on your height and age. All inhabitants of Planet Six eat this."

I took a slurp. It tasted like paste. I know because I'd tasted paste before. Once was enough. "And what of flavor?"

His head remained tilted. "Again, all inhabitants eat the same, no variation. Equal portions per meal, based on height and age, provided by the government in exchange for services rendered."

"What kind of services."

"Jobs, I believe you would call them."

I shrugged. I ate. I needed, as he put it, nutrition. Maybe, I hoped, there were restaurants with better options, but I wasn't bothering to cross my fingers in that regard.

"So, everyone is equal on this planet?"

"It is the law, Randy."

I looked at the bare room, the bare floor, the bare bed. "And everyone is happy?"

He shrugged. "Another subjective term."

I thought of the houses, the buildings, the formality of it all, the lack of warmth. I thought of Milo's home. It was decorated without flare, without personality, individuality.

"Art," I said, staring at the white, metal wall. "What of art?"

"Also subjective and nonexistent. An art piece would be appreciated by some, not all. All would need to appreciate it."

"Equally."

He nodded. "It is the law."

I nodded. I got it. Everyone was equal in every regard. Milo had said there were no divisions of race or gender or sexuality. Equal. All equal. I stuck my tongue out at the bare wall. "Boring Planet Six." I turned to Tag. "Do they have orgies on this planet."

"If so desired, Randy."

I smiled. "Okay, so it's a little less boring." I got dressed. I slid my jumpsuit on. I froze when I saw the card that still dangled off the grey material. There had been a light on it that glowed yellow; it now glowed blue.

I looked up at Tag. "What happened to it."

"Your government-issued card has been deactivated."

"Because we broke the law? Because it was stolen?"

"Presumably."

I frowned. That, apart from Tag, had been our one saving grace. We could hide with it, go where we needed to go. Now what would we do? "Can you fix it, Tag?"

He scanned the card. "It is illegal to fix. Protected."

"Uh-huh, and *so* not what I was asking you."

He gazed up at me, those green eyes surprisingly alive with wonder, with curiosity. Was this simply technology, programming for my benefit? It was funny, actually, this whole Tag thing. I honestly thought of him as my friend now. Was it because I'd see him naked, blue bush and all? Or was it something else, like maybe because I needed all the friends I could get?

"Milo would never ask you to do such a thing, something illegal?"

"Doubtful, though Milo did break the law when he communicated with you, so it is not outside the realm of possibility, however improbable it might be that he would ask."

My gut tightened. *For me*, Tag had said. Milo had broken the law for me. *He's in trouble because of me.*

"You care about him, about Milo?" I asked.

"Milo is my friend. I care, as you put it, for his well-being."

"And so do I. Which is why I'm asking you to break the law."

He nodded. The colors of the light changed as they shot from my wrist and hit the ID card, morphing between yellow and red and orange and back again. He was doing as I asked, staring at his work as I in turn stared at him. "Are you...are you self-aware, Tag?"

He briefly gazed my way. "I am active, Randy. My device is powered on."

"Again, not the question."

"Then I do not understand the question."

I nodded. I thought of another way to phrase it. I took the watch off my wrist, though it continued to emit its colorful rays. "If I smashed this, destroyed it, you would cease to exist."

He nodded, his face in a strangely rueful configuration. "I would prefer you did not do that, Randy."

I smiled. "That answered my question, Tag. Thank you."

Again, he locked eyes with me. "You do not ask questions like others do, Randy. You do not make requests like others."

"And you like that?"

He shrugged. The beams of light vanished. "The card is fixed. It will function as before, though no longer registered to the previous owner, and so, in theory, it is now untraceable. If you are caught, I will be deactivated. You will be incarcerated." He smiled. "And yes, I, as you say, *like* that."

My smile matched his. "You like that because we're friends."

He nodded. "Yes, because we are friends."

I went to hug him, and then thought the better of it. Instead, I bade him to follow. "Great. Now, let's go scare the shit out of Craig."

"Sounds messy, Randy."

I laughed. "Yes, it does, doesn't it?"

Chapter 7

Craig did not appreciate the shit scared out of him, which is what made it so much fun. It was, in fact, like being back home—minus, of course, the friendly hologram.

In any case, I filled him in on what I'd learned about the planet, about Tag, though not what Milo and Tag looked like while fucking. He nodded as he ate his paste. He looked none too happy with it. I knew the feeling—though not the taste, seeing as it had none.

Now that we were all caught up, I turned to Tag. "So, where was Milo last seen?"

Tag blinked. "A quarter Earth mile from here. Would you like to keep me in this mode and follow?"

"It won't look weird out in public?" I asked.

He shook his head. "Not common, but not unheard of either. If we see people, they will not care or be alarmed, if that is your concern."

I nodded. Craig nodded. "Let's go then, dude."

"Dude?" said Tag.

I grinned. "Pet name."

"But I am no pet," said Tag.

I shook my head. "It's how friends refer to other friends. It replaces the use of the person's name. Craig is hooked on it. He thinks it makes him sound cool."

A breeze suddenly blew from the watch. "I can make that happen as well."

I laughed. I walked us out of the apartment. I dropped the English lesson; it was more laborious than it was worth. We then followed Tag down the hall and out of the building.

The sun was bright as it jutted above the distant horizon, its rays bouncing off the buildings that surrounded us, making everything appear a warm orange. I breathed in. It smelled fresh. It didn't smell like any city I'd ever been in before.

Craig pointed down the street. "People."

There were two people, in fact, so at least we were finally no longer alone. And, thankfully, they weren't in grey jumpsuits, nor were they chasing us. I turned around and stared in the other direction. There were three more people. So, there were now five people in our general vicinity. Five people in a massive city. It made no sense. Still, at least we had easy access to the streets and people movers, which meant that we'd find Milo all that much quicker.

Tag led us to one of those people movers, which promptly got us going in the right direction. And so, we moved as Craig and I looked around. There were no businesses, but with all the windows and doors hidden from sight, who could tell? I guessed you just had to know where you were going, or have your watch tell you, or maybe everything simply got delivered to you. Maybe Amazon finally achieved world domination—or perhaps other-world, as was the case. Or maybe the planet's inhabitants really did eat nothing but nutritious paste and wore the same clothes year in and year out, changing the colors of said clothes as they saw fit.

Lost in my thoughts, I didn't realize that we'd arrived. Tag exited the people mover, even though he wasn't technically, um, *people*; technically, he was nothing more than, um, technology, and a holographic version at that.

The three of us then stood side by side, staring at the building in front of us, at the last known whereabouts of Milo. Said building was short and squat, unlike the skyscrapers around it, but, like them, it had no windows or doors, no signage.

"What is it?" I asked.

"Odd," replied Tag.

We both looked at him. "Odd?" I echoed. "It's like all the other buildings we've seen, except for the size and shape."

He looked at me. "Odd, in that it's not registering. Milo's body GPS pinned him to this spot, but this spot doesn't show up in the system. It has no name, no function. It is, as if, it doesn't exist."

Craig pointed at the building. "*It* begs to differ."

I tapped Tag's shoulder. I swiped air. I'd have to remember not to do that; it was disconcerting, to say the least. "Perhaps it's a secret government building then."

"The government has no secrets," Tag said.

I shook my head. "Unless *that's* the secret."

We continued standing there. I suppose we were waiting for one of us to come up with a brilliant idea, preferably Tag. Eventually, two men came out of the building both in—surprise, surprise—grey jumpsuits.

"Think that proves it?" I asked.

Craig shook his head. "They could just as easily be janitors or mechanics, according to what Tag told us."

Tag nodded. "But they're not."

I cocked an eye his way. I wondered why you could cock your eye, but not your nose or your mouth. Heck, you didn't even cock your cock. "How do you know that?" I asked him.

He pointed to the watch. "Listen," he said. He cranked up the sound, the watch, apparently, picking up the conversation of the two men. Given that there were no other noises anywhere, it wasn't all that surprising that we could hear them, or that the watch was also a listening device. Given that it could project a hologram—and a sexy hologram at that—I wasn't surprised that it could do anything that it could do. Heck, you could probably shove carrots into it and get juice. If this planet had any vegetables, that is. If this planet had any food besides paste.

And so, we listened intently as the watch simultaneously translated. When they were finally out of range, we all looked at each other.

"Government prison," I said. "What makes this different from a regular prison?" Tag shrugged, and so I added, "*Earth watch*, they kept saying. Is that the name of a company, an experiment, what?"

"There is no official organization known by that name," Tag replied.

"And unofficial?" I asked.

He nodded. "Checking gossip news." There was a brief pause. "Earth-Watch, one word, hyphenated, is an underground organization that has been studying your planet since the universes converged."

"Milo told me that your planet had been monitoring ours," I said. "That wasn't a secret. He said it was like watching TV, except that your people got bored with us and changed the channel years ago. So, what's different about these guys?"

Tag turned and looked at me. My cock twitched every time our eyes locked. With his halo of light and sparkling pools of green, it was like gazing at an angel. In fact, I now knew what a moth felt like when it encountered a flame. *Pfft!* What a brilliant way to go. Then again, a moth never crashed into a watch. "It's all rumor, conjecture, but Earth-Watch purportedly means to utilize your species in order to save our own. They might have already infiltrated your planet, in fact. Impossible to say, seeing as, officially, they don't exist."

"Wait, what?" I said.

"They don't exist," he repeated.

"No, back up," I said.

"To which part?"

I sighed. *Really? The part you glossed over, you stupid hologram.* "The part about using our species to save yours. Save your species from what?"

To which Craig added, and wisely so, "And utilize us how?"

I nodded. "Milo promised: no dissecting, no anal probes."

Tag did that head tilt he did when he hadn't a clue what I was talking about. "How would anal probing help us? Is this some strange Earth custom?"

Craig chuckled and aimed his brow my way. "For some."

I shook my head. "Anyway, back to our questions, please."

Tag looked around, then pointed around. "I thought you knew."

"Knew? Knew what? I still don't know!" I shouted. I looked at Craig. "Do you know?"

He squinted up at the sky. He, too, looked around. He scratched his chin, and then looked back my way. "Eight hundred people in this city," he said, and Tag nodded. "There used to be more, though, right?"

"Six million or so."

"What?" I said. "Six million? When was this? Where did they all go?"

"Dead," Tag said.

"Dead?" I said. "Killed, all at the same time? By what, a meteor, a virus, enemy planet?" I had several more movie options, all of them starring Tom Cruise, but I was suddenly out of breath.

"No," said Tag. "Old age, I suppose. Most of them, anyway." He looked at Craig. He looked at me. "It's been more than seven hundred years, so the data is, as you say, sketchy."

My eyes went from looking at Tag to looking at Craig. "Lost, little bro."

He nodded. "You told me that Milo told you that the difference between our species and his, at least from a genetic standpoint, is an extra sex chromosome, namely Z. But I'm guessing there's more to it than that."

Tag nodded knowingly, a frown quickly giving chase. "Your Y chromosome, it has few active genes, especially as compared to the rest of your chromosomal makeup. Ours, however, no longer has any, hence the evolvement of the Z chromosome. In time, your Y chromosome will lose all function, but that time is millions of years into your future."

"Wait," I said. "From what little I know about genetics, which is slight, at best, only males have Y chromosomes. So, no Y chromosomes, no males. No males, no babies."

Tag again nodded. "It's a simplistic explanation, but yes, more or less."

"My brother does simplistic well," Craig interjected. "But there are people here. Few, it seems, but people just the same."

Tag sighed, which was strange, seeing as he had no lungs. "Genetic mutation. The Z chromosome, for a rare select few, enables births, seeing as it evolved from the Y. As the latter was in its death throes, the former was given life. Ergo, we are still a species."

"Ergo!" shouted Craig.

"Oh God," I sighed—after all, I do have lungs. "Not that again."

"Lost me," said Tag.

"Welcome to the club," said I. "Anyway, what does all that have to do with us? Us humans, I mean?"

"The other planets in our solar system, Planets Three, Four and Six, all have similar problems."

It was then I understood. I mean, I might be slow on the uptake, but I eventually suck it all in, so to speak. "Twenty-plus years ago, our two universes aligned, connected, still connect, even if only for short periods at a time. We, therefore, are your closest neighbor with a similar genetic makeup and a working Y chromosome."

"Bingo," said Craig.

"And this Earth-Watch? They mean to take advantage of this, while the getting's good?"

"What's a getting?" Tag asked.

"Never mind," I said. "But how does Milo fit into all this?"

Craig raised his hand. "This planet has a no-contact law. Milo made contact. Milo, potentially, ruined their plans. We know about them now. We could, in theory, prepare for an invasion, if that is their goal. We know where the contact point is, the portal. We could amass an army in San Francisco. They're stronger by far, but far fewer in number, too. We could, most likely, annihilate them, if need be."

Tag's nodding returned. "That would all make sense. If such an organization does exist, and if they were planning to utilize your genetic makeup to enhance our own, Milo's indiscretion could lay waste to their plans."

"But I'm barely out of college, and a mediocre college at that, and still living with his parents," I said by way of an objection. "Who would believe me? Plus, until this very moment, I didn't even know any of this."

"But they don't know that," said Craig. "And, even if they did, in time, Milo could've told you more, perhaps tipped you off, even if you're not so easily tipped."

I grimaced. "Must you?"

He smiled. "Oh, I must." He looked at Tag again. "If we crossed through the portal, then it's possible for others to do the same, through different portals. Do you think they've already done so, put their plan into action?"

Tag shrugged. "No idea. As far as the databases are saying, this organization doesn't even exist. As to what they're planning, what they've accomplished, that's impossible to say. Unless…"

Craig pointed at the squat building in front of us. "Unless, we get inside there."

"And rescue Milo," I added.

They both nodded. I nodded right along with them. We suddenly looked like a trio of bobbleheads.

"Well?" I asked. "Any ideas?"

Craig pointed at me. "You have the government-issued outfit and security card. I can't get in without the latter. And I'm guessing there are sensors that would prevent me from piggy-backing inside with you."

My heart began to lub-dub in double-time. "So, you're saying I should go in there all by myself?"

Craig reached over and tapped the watch. "Not alone."

"I'll be with you the entire time," Tag said reassuringly. Though I wasn't reassured. I knew the Tag standing next to me was only just a hologram, even if he felt real to me. Which meant, if I went in there, I'd be on my own—me, the guy who didn't even like to go to the mall by himself.

And so, I did the smart thing. "Here," I said to Craig, handing him the security card. "You go."

"But I'm only eighteen," objected Craig.

"And he looks even younger," said Tag. "Fifteen, maybe."

"Hey!" objected Craig.

I sighed. This wasn't getting us anywhere. And the truth of the matter was that Milo was in there. I felt it, felt it even stronger now, probably since we were so close to him now. It was as if I had a collar on, and a leash was being pulled, yanking me toward him. In other words, I knew I had to go in.

I turned to Craig. "You'll be alone if I go inside." He nodded my way. "And I'll need Tag." He nodded again. "I…I don't like leaving you, little bro. This world looks safe and all, but we stole these outfits; they're after us now."

"We came to rescue Milo," he said, shaking his head. "Go and rescue Milo; I'll be fine."

Our eyes locked. Mom and Dad would kill me if I let anything happen to him. I'd probably kill me, too. But what choice did I have? He was right; we came to rescue Milo. "I'll be back in an hour. You stay here. If I don't make it back, try and find the portal, then tell Mom and Dad that I—"

He held up his hand. "You're getting all schmaltzy on me, dude," he said. "You'll be fine. I'll see you in an hour. I won't move. Besides, that paste breakfast is hardening in my stomach even as we speak; I couldn't move even if I wanted to." He patted his belly and burped. "Maybe it wasn't that fucked up Y chromosome that killed off these people, after all."

I grinned. I frowned. This was awful. Seriously, awful. I turned to Tag. I pointed at the watch. "Time to put the genie back in the bottle."

He seemed to understand the reference. He shimmered for the briefest of moments before disappearing. The watch vibrated on my wrist, pulsed, lit up. "I've scanned the building, Randy. There are multiple areas that don't appear. One would assume that Milo is being held in one of those areas."

I nodded. I gulped. I began to walk toward the building.

"Good luck, dude," Craig said.

And still I nodded. And still I gulped. My heart felt like it could give the Energizer Bunny a run for its money. I didn't turn around to look at Craig. I knew that if I did, I'd probably chicken out. And bunnies don't do chicken. So, I walked, acting as if I belonged there. I then smiled just before I stepped inside, mainly because it hit me that I was an alien, a little green man, so to speak. They were probably more afraid of me than I was of them, right? Right? Yeah, I know. Not a chance.

The wall slid open. There were no alarms, no bells, no whistles. I was sure I'd been scanned, but nothing seemed amiss. You know, apart from an alien intruder entering a secret government building. An alien intruder looking to rescue a Planet-Sixian that said alien intruder had never officially met before.

I walked further in. There was no front desk, no receptionist. There was simply a lobby, a couple of chairs off to the side, several signs along the wall, and no doors, as per usual. There were also no people. At least not yet.

"Thoughts?" I said in a whisper as I stood there staring ahead, a sign in front, a sign on my left, a sign on my right. Talk about your crossroads. They say to pick the road less travelled, but, well…

"There's a dark area on the right and on the left, according to my building scan. Ahead, I can scan the entire region. If Milo is here, he must be on the right or the left." There was the briefest of pauses before he added, "And, Randy, this building is heavily fortified, armed; that I can also see in the scan."

"Fuck," I spat. "Now you tell me." I looked at the watch. "Can you counterattack?"

"With what? A laser beam? I think the human phrase would be: *give me a break.*"

I sighed. "Yes, that would be the correct phrase."

I looked left. I looked right. The wall looked the same either way, the signs in a language I clearly couldn't read. Even if I could, it wouldn't help me. And so, I closed my eyes and simply breathed. I listened to my heart, waiting for it to tell me where to go. *Which door?* I said to myself. *Which door?* I gripped my hands. I squeezed tightly. My chest did the same to the pumping organ within, as if to pry loose the answer. *Which door?*

"Left," I finally uttered, that leash again tugging as my eyelids fluttered open.

"You sure?" said Tag.

I looked down. "Nope."

I turned left as I shrugged. Well, no. Actually, I turned left after I prayed, then I shrugged. I hoped God was listening, that he knew who I was, what with me so far from home, and all. Then I put one foot in front of the other, my body on autopilot, legs moving even as my brain froze, as that pumping heart of mine revved, threatening to burst from pressure.

The wall silently parted open. There was a hallway. There were rooms. There were strange objects I had no point of reference for. They could have been weapons. They could have been pieces of luggage. They could have been anything. They weren't Milo, though, and so I simply glanced at them and kept moving.

I saw a few people. One was at the end of the hall. One was in a room to my right. One was in a different room to my right. He looked like he was monitoring something, but the screen wasn't facing my way. None of the three seemed to pay me much heed. All looked at me, saw the grey jumpsuit, the security badge, and promptly ignored me. *Phew.*

I kept moving. I nodded to the man in the hallway as I passed him. He nodded back. He said something I couldn't understand. I replied in a mutter as I quickened my step. I reached another wall. I whispered into the watch. "What did he say?"

"Good morning."

"Nice fellow."

"He had a weapon on him that could annihilate your San Francisco with a single press of a button."

My gulp returned, bulging my throat. "Oh."

"The wall you're standing in front of, this is also an area I can't scan. All I see is black, black until I reach the end of the building. It's a large space. Two stories. But that's all I can tell. There might be a few people back there, there might be many dozens, all with similar weapons to that man back there."

That gulp of mine threatened to rupture the dam. "Your bedside manner leaves something to be desired, Tag."

"I don't understand."

"Clearly."

My foot moved forward. The wall parted. I felt like Moses. *Please don't let the Egyptians be right behind me.* Though, of course, it was what was in front that I should've been worried about.

Chapter 8

The wall closed behind me. I jumped, despite the silence of it. I wanted to ask Tag to scan the area again, to look for Milo, now that we were on the other side, but I wasn't alone. In fact, unlike the rest of the city, the space we were in teemed with people, easily a couple of dozen, men and women, all of them stunningly attractive. Yippy for that Z chromosome. Not so yippy for me, though, because several of them quickly approached.

They held their palms my way. Apparently, the sign for *halt* was universal. They spoke. Planet-Sixian, by the way, was clearly not a romance language. It sounded a lot like German, only less, um, romantic. I froze. A deer caught in the headlights was more animate. In other words, when they stopped speaking and were clearly waiting for a reply, I just stood there staring.

Eventually, when I didn't say anything and they didn't say anything, I realized it was my turn to speak. FYI, I knew I couldn't do that. If I spoke English, all hope was lost—for me, for Milo, perhaps for my entire species. I mean, if they could blow up a city with the press of a button, imagine what they could do to an entire planet. Or don't imagine it. Because it's not a pretty picture. I know because I was, in fact, picturing it.

Anyway, I pointed at my watch. You know, animatedly. With gusto. *Point, point, point*, I went.

Tag, thank goodness, took the hint and began to reply in their language. I assumed he told them that I was from Planet Four, that I was a mute, that he would answer any and all questions. I assumed all this, though none of it seemed to matter.

That is to say, they didn't welcome me with open arms. Not unless the custom on their planet was to grab you and drag you around—and rather roughly, I might add—before they threw your ass in a cell. The bars were made of beams of light, which I could only assume would slice you in half should you decide to try and escape through them. And no, I wasn't eager to prove my theory correct.

So, not ten minutes after I entered the building, I was in jail. *Nice job, Randy.*

I looked down at the watch, and whispered, "What happened?"

"Facial recognition," he replied. "Your face was scanned when you stole the card at the station. As soon as you walked inside the building, they knew it. Thankfully, thus far, they don't know exactly who you are."

"Wait," I said. "Why didn't you warn me about the facial stuff before?"

"I didn't know they utilized the technology. This is a secret government building. This must be a secret government practice. Makes sense."

"Uh-huh," I said. "Great for them."

"I'm sorry, Randy," he said.

I sighed and sunk my head to my chest. There was a bed and a chair in there. I sat down. "It wasn't your fault, Tag. You didn't know. I took the risk. It simply didn't pay off." *Now what? Now what's going to happen to me, to us?* I thought of Craig. What would he do now, alone on a strange planet? My stomach knotted at the thought. I fucked up. I fucked up badly.

I started to cry, but I was interrupted mid-sniffle.

They say that when God closes a door, he opens a window. Seems that jail cells have windows, too.

"Randy?" I heard from the cell adjoining mine.

A man rose from the bed.

My body went rigid. Everywhere. Literally. "Milo?"

I jumped from my chair. He jumped from his.

"What are you doing here?" he asked, his face an inch from mine, the beams the only thing in the way. Amazingly, he was even more stunning in person. It was, in fact, like meeting Michelangelo's *David*.

"Badly," I replied. "Doing badly. FYI, you shouldn't steal on Planet Six."

"Or communicate with handsome aliens."

I nodded. He nodded. He stared into my eyes. I stared into his. An epic novel was written within that stare.

Eventually, he blinked. "But how did you get here?" He whispered this last part. I hoped it was enough, that they weren't recording us, listening in. I mean, they were monitoring my face, so why not my voice? In any case, there were no guards, just a bunch of cells, half of them empty. I tended to think guards would be overkill, just like the bar-beams themselves. I mean, there's dying and then there's being sliced like a Christmas ham dying. Even standing that close to them gave me the heebie-jeebies, made the hairs on my arms stand on end.

I held my finger to my lips. I hoped he got the suggestion. "Later," I said.

"Later," he said wistfully. "I hope we get a later."

"Do you know why you're here?" I asked.

He nodded. He shook his head. "To a degree. Though only mostly that I broke the law."

I frowned. "And your punishment?"

His nod turned shrug. "They won't answer me when I ask. I take it by the surroundings that it won't be good."

"And me? I stole this snazzy jumpsuit. What's the punishment for bad taste?"

He pointed to my security card. "I think *that's* your problem, Randy."

I gulped. "That bad?"

He nodded. "That bad. You don't fuck with the government. They take care of us, but demand total obedience in return. Crime, any crime, is a no-no. Which means, I can't even begin to imagine what they have in store for us."

"So, we need to escape then."

He pointed to the bars. "How?"

I pointed to Tag. I smiled. "Secret weapon."

"Tag? Tag's no secret. He was a birthday present from my parents."

"*Shh*," I shushed him. "He's got feelings, too."

Milo shot me a *you've got to be kidding me* look. "You've got to be kidding me." See!

"No, really. He does," I said. "He has feelings, just like you and me."

"He's a program."

I shook my head. "A program with feelings." I thought about a better word for it. I came up with two. "Self-preservation." Or is that one word? "Self-preservation." Yes, I think it's hyphenated. Does that make it one word or two? Anyway, I said, "He'd prefer it if we didn't destroy him."

Milo sighed. Even that was stunning. "Because he's expensive."

"No, because he…well, just take my word for it. Anyway, he'll get us out of this."

Tag blinked. That is to say, Tag pulsed on my arm. "Maybe," he said.

I stared down at my wrist. Milo did the same. "Maybe?" we both said in unison. "It was a yes or no type of question, Tag," I added. "Can you help us escape or can't you?"

Again, he blinked. "Maybe."

"That's annoying," I said.

"Yep," agreed Milo. "He does that sometimes."

I wagged my finger Milo's way and managed a wry smile. "Sounds more like a person than a program."

He sighed, yet again, and lifted his hands as if to say *I give*. Seems that was universal as well. "In any case, Tag," I said, again looking down at my wrist, "why only maybe?"

"Because I'll either free you or kill you. If I kill you, then it's a moot point if you're free at the time. Hence, maybe."

"Hence?" said Milo.

"Better than ergo," I said.

"Huh?"

"Never mind." I looked at my wrist again. "Probabilities here, Tag?"

"Approximately thirty/seventy, Randy," he replied. "The odds being in your favor."

Again, Milo and I locked eyes, a thousand butterflies instantly swarming in my belly. I came to rescue him; I still meant to do just that. Besides, I was a dead man either way, or whatever these people had in mind for me.

"I'm game," I said.

He shrugged. "Sure, why not?"

Tag pulsed on my arm. "That was easy."

Again, Milo shrugged. "What choice did we have?" He gazed down at my wrist. "So, what's the plan?"

I felt my wrist suddenly vibrate. The watch was shaking, trembling. "What are you doing, Tag?" I asked.

"Disassociating," he replied.

"Disassociating what?" I replied. At that, the glass surface of him popped off and landed with a *clink* on the floor. "Oh." I bent down and retrieved it. "Now what?"

"The glass," said Milo. "It's scratchproof, shatterproof, virtually indestructible."

Instantly, I understood the plan. "Laser-proof?"

To which Tag replied. "No, not exactly."

"Explain," said Milo.

"The bars that surround you are generated by a powerful laser emitter. The beams can cut through most objects, the glass in Randy's hand included. Still, the glass will reflect the beams, perhaps for a few seconds, before it shatters."

I nodded. "And a few seconds is all we need."

Milo joined my nod with one of his own. "So, where does the probability of death figure in to all this?"

"Randy will hold the glass," Tag replied, my eyed wide at the prospect of holding such a small object up close to the beams. I needed my fingers, after all. I liked them, in fact. They came in, you know, *handy*. "But I won't know the exact angle the glass is held at, so I can't calculate the trajectory. Or, as will most certainly be the case, trajectories, plural."

My hands, like the watch previously, began to tremble. "The glass will act as a prism, not a mirror," I said.

"That is correct, Randy."

"And, since we're in these cells, we'll be in the path of said trajectories," I lamented. "In which case, how is it that we only have a thirty percent chance of dying?" Oh, that word. Not a nice word. Not when you're in a cell, surrounded by laser beams, on a strange planet that feeds you nothing but paste.

"The glass," said Tag, "is coated with a strong metal on the bottom, which protects my inner workings. The beam will, therefore, only be diverted upward, once you inject the glass through it. You, at the time, will be crouching downward. The resulting light show should then be above your head."

To which Milo asked, "So, apart from being both potentially pretty and/or deadly, how will we be able to escape, post-glass-insertion?"

"The beams are projected downward from the ceiling, Milo. Each cell is on its own circuit, which means that you can switch each of them on and off separately. Still, all the cells are on the same system. Take out the system, and all the cells will be switched off."

I smiled at the ingenuity, forgetting, however temporarily, that I could soon be dead, that we could all, in fact, be gruesomely dead. "And one, if not all the refracted beams, will, hopefully, take out the system."

Tag's lights flashed. "Exactly."

To which Milo then asked, "Then why is the probability still so high that we might die?" I cringed at the word. The *die* part.

"Numerous reasons," replied Tag. "The two most likely are: the ceiling, or part of it, could collapse on top of you; or there could be a security system installed that will react to our plan in a way that results in your demise. The latter seems the most probable. Though you could potentially also die from smoke inhalation or fire, should you be trapped in this room after the plan is completed."

I looked at Milo. "His program clearly doesn't include sugarcoating."

Milo shrugged. "If you say so." And then he smiled my way, apparently trying to reassure me. I wasn't reassured, but I smiled back, just the same—and okay, sprang a bit of a boner. Because I might've been near death, but I was still barely in my twenties and, as always, the little head ruled the big one.

"Ready?" Milo asked as he crouched as low to the ground as he could get.

"Nope," I replied, also crouching. "But let's do it."

Milo leaned his face up and shouted something in his own language. He then turned to me and said, "I told the other prisoners to duck or risk certain painful death and/or dismemberment."

"More and, than or." I peeked above his head. The other prisoners, which looked like five in total, were all now similarly crouching. I then held the glass, metal down, near one of the beams. "It was a pleasure meeting you, Milo."

He smiled. My dick throbbed. "Save the pleasure for later, Randy. After we get the hell out of here."

I nodded, sweat forming on my forehead before trickling down. I inched the glass forward, my heartrate tripling in an instant. Closer it went, closer still, edging it and us closer to our destinies. And then, there it was, the glass slicing the beam from below, refracting from above, sending out shafts of brilliant orange in all directions.

"Pretty," I made note.

FYI, it was indeed pretty, for all of about two seconds. Then nuh-uh, not even close. Thankfully—and trust me, that word doesn't even almost fit what befell us after those two pretty seconds—in any case, *thankfully*, the ceiling did not cave in on us. It smoked, sure, and fizzled, yep, and crumpled a little, hell to the yeah, but, then again, so did everything else in that room.

First off, after the beams scattered, they did in fact hit some sort of main system. I know this because all the laser bars in the room promptly flickered and died. Cheers went up from the other inmates. Cheers went up from me and Milo, too, as we crouched there, praying we wouldn't cave in, or smoke and fizzle, or crumple like the rest of the room was doing all around us, which was loudly and with a great many sparks, mainly owing to the fact that the building was built entirely of metal. FYI, in case you didn't know it, metal stinks something awful when its bombarded with insanely strong laser beams. Holes in the ceiling formed. Holes in the walls followed suit. Like I said, the ceiling didn't collapse, but it did begin to melt, molten metal dripping down in giant globs of orange as the room quickly filled with smoke and stink and the grating sound of alarms, which also seemed to be universal. In other words, Planet Six alarms were no more pleasant to the ears than Earth ones.

I coughed. Milo did the same. Tag, of course, did not. "Run!" my watch shouted. "And grab some weapons! They're by the front door, hanging from the wall!"

I ran. It seemed to be a good suggestion. Milo grabbed my hand. I turned to look at him, locking in on his eyes of blue as sparks sparked at the periphery and smoke clouded my sight. I coughed again, even as I smiled. All in all, if you had to die, what an awesome way to go.

We found the weapons. I grabbed a handful and shoved them in my jumpsuit pockets. They were small, though I was guessing powerful. Milo grabbed a couple of them, too. The other prisoners followed suit, amassing behind us. I walked to the wall. The door slid open. Chaos was reigning supreme in the hallway, men and women running to and fro, the smoke even denser out there, the alarms jarringly loud.

I sped ahead, a weapon in one hand, Milo's hand in the other. I was panting from fear all the while. I hadn't a clue how to fire the thing, the weapon, that is. Heck, it looked like a cell phone. Maybe I could blast a hole in the front of the building and call home at the same time.

I was hacking from the smoke now, tears streaming down my face, heart pounding in my ears even louder than the alarms. And still I gripped the weapon and Milo as if my life depended on it. Which it, you know, did. Like, duh.

We ran to the end of the hall. By then, it was too smoky to make us out, for the guards to be able to tell who were the good guys and who were the bad ones. We ran and kept on running as the front wall parted and out we flew, a plume of black rising above us before wafting to the sky.

I pointed ahead with the weapon. "There!" I shouted. "Craig is waiting for us!"

"You brought your little brother with you?!"

I grinned even as the tears stung my eyes. "Actually, he brought me." I turned to him as I winked away the salt. "Long story."

We found him a few minutes later. He was sitting against the building we'd left him at, picking his cuticles. He was around the corner. He couldn't see the inferno we'd left behind, plus the wind was blowing the smoke in the opposite direction. In other words, he hadn't a clue how heroic I'd been. Damn.

He looked up and smiled. "That was quick. Must've been easy." He stood. He shook Milo's hand. I wasn't too happy about that, mainly because Milo had to let go of my hand to return the shake. "Prison life treat you well? You look, um, *sooty*." He suddenly stared around us, beyond us. "And you brought me a girl. Thanks, but I didn't get you anything."

Our heads whipped around. There was indeed a girl standing behind us. She must've been a fellow prisoner, though she looked no older than seventeen, eighteen, maybe. I wondered what she could've done to land herself in such an awful place.

Milo talked to her as we watched. And speaking of watched, Tag again appeared by our side, looking far better than Milo or I did. I thought to hug him, but, well, you know. I looked at the device on my wrist. "You need a new piece of glass."

He nodded. "Just don't spill water on me until then."

I smiled. "Deal." I turned to Milo. He was still talking to the girl. "Come on," I said, again grabbing his hand. It gave me peace. It gave me comfort. It gave me a woody. "We should go; they'll be looking for us all too soon."

Tag lifted his holographic finger. "I infiltrated their database while the lightshow was going on. I altered your face in their systems. They can no longer find you that way."

We started moving again. "You think of everything," I said.

Milo chuckled. "He better; he cost enough."

Tag ran along with us. It was an odd sight to see, a hologram running and glowing. "You're welcome," he said to Milo.

Again, Milo laughed, the sound magical to my ears. "Okay, okay. Thanks. And good to see you, old friend."

We rounded a bend. The alarms that had been going off inside the government building were now blaring in the streets. They were indeed after us, I figured. I pointed to a building. "In there," I said. "They can't spot us if they can't see us."

I still had my ID card attached to my jumpsuit. The building welcomed us with open arms. In we ran, the wall silently sliding shut. The four of us stood in the entryway. Introductions were officially made.

The girl was named Britney. Actually, the girl wasn't named Britney, but she looked like Ms. Spears in her younger years, and her actual name was as difficult to pronounce as Milo's, and so Britney it was. Britney was arrested for hacking into the government's databases.

She'd discovered Earth-Watch. She'd been arrested a week before Milo.

"Her parents must be worried sick," I said.

Milo frowned. And still he looked glorious. "No parents. Orphaned. Girls aren't treasured on our planet. Boys are the key to our survival."

"Awful," I said. "And where does she live then?"

"Government housing." His frown sagged farther. "Many girls find themselves there. Apparently, they have excellent 'computer equipment,' as you would call it. It would seem that the girls are allowed free rein on it." He pointed at Britney. "Case in point."

She smiled coyly. She was beautiful, just like the rest of her species. She was also eyeing my brother like a coyote would a chicken. Not surprisingly, Craig was thrilled at the attention—very unlike a chicken, which would generally cluck and run away; Craig, suffice it to say, did neither.

"I need to rest a bit," I said.

"Same," said Milo.

Craig shrugged. "I'm good."

I sighed as we found an elevator and quickly rose to the top floor. Tag found us two empty apartments. It wasn't difficult; they were all empty. I handed Craig the watch. "Keep an eye on them, Tag," I said.

Tag tilted his glowing head. "Sounds painful. If, that is, I had a real eye."

I grinned. "Yeah, whatever."

Milo and I disappeared into our apartment before the conversation could continue. The wall closed behind us. I turned. Milo turned. Our lips were pressed together before I could inhale. Instead, I exhaled into his lungs as my soul was set aflame, as fireworks burst from behind my eyelids, as every nerve ending in my body was simultaneously set off.

This being my first kiss, I had nothing to compare it to, but still I'd wager that it was, as kisses went, incomparable. Perfect, in fact.

Heavenly. Though I was glad we'd missed the trip there, if just by a hair—to heaven, that is to say. Because then I'd miss out on that kiss, and the one to follow, and the one to follow that, the kisses melding and meshing—not to mention mashing—into one fabulously long lip-lock that, for all I cared, could've lasted until the end of time.

"Hi," he eventually said as we at last came up for air, as he stroked my cheek, smiling brightly all the while.

I stared into all that sparkling blue, very much mesmerized. "Hi," I echoed as my heart thumped madly away. "You look better on this side of the mirror."

"To quote your kind, *ditto*."

I was engulfed within his warm embrace. Milo did great embrace. "Speaking of my kind," I said. "Yours means to somehow utilize our genetic makeup, to help solve your Y/Z chromosome problem. You made contact with me. You potentially could've ruined this plan of theirs. You were jailed as a result."

He sighed. "Bad me." The sigh was followed by yet another brightening smile, the kind that toothpaste commercials are made of. "But what is their plan?"

I shrugged. "Beats me."

He squinted his eyes. "Beat you? You enjoy pain, Randy?"

I laughed. It felt good to laugh. Surreal, given the circumstances, but still. "It's an Earth expression. It means: I don't have a clue."

"And what are *your* plans?"

My shrug saw my previous shrug and raised it a wink. "Beats me."

"Sounds sexual, if you ask me."

My wink promptly folded. "Um, really?" I squeaked out.

He looked around. "Well, we do have the apartment to ourselves."

Hell, we had practically the entire city to ourselves. In any case, I moved to a couch. It was grey. It was Earth-couch-like. It was functional, but without beauty. "I, um, yeah…"

He sat next to me. I'd waited for this moment for so long now.

Not just with Milo, but, you know, in general. I was twenty-two. Most people I knew weren't virgins anymore, not even close. I was super horny, sure, but super scared as well. Plus, I was with a super alien.

"My body parts are just like yours," he said, his hand placed over mine.

I looked down at said hand. "It's not that." Mostly. I mean, I'd already seen him as a hologram and knew that he didn't have two dicks, that he didn't have a veritable anaconda hidden inside his slacks, that he didn't have cubes instead of balls. But no, those weren't my concerns. Again, mostly. "I've, uh, never been with a man before?"

"But there are men all over your planet. Your father is a man. Surely, you've been with men."

I sighed. "*Been* been."

He shrugged. "I think my English studies were inadequate."

My sigh repeated. My dick, miraculously, remained rock-solid. "Sexually. I've never been with a man sexually." I forced a smile. Or maybe I'd already been smiling all the while. It was hard, no pun intended, to know. "You were the first person I ever kissed."

He squinted my way. "Also, to quote your kind, *no fucking way.*"

I chuckled nervously. "Your English studies were more than adequate, Milo." Same for the dude sitting next to me, who was way, way more than adequate. I mean, seriously, way. "It's just, it never felt quite right...before."

He smiled. He leaned in, his lips pressed to mine. I felt the air as it exhaled from his nose onto my upper lip. He squeezed my hand. "Humans," he uttered, his face an inch from my own. "Do they believe in this concept of fate?"

I shrugged. "Some do, some don't. Planet-Sixians?"

He laughed. I felt the rumble of it down my spine. "Cureans. We are known as Cureans. We speak Cureal. The first being on our planet was called Curea. In your mythos, he would've been known as Adam." His grin widened. "I believe in fate, Randy. Our worlds aligned in our bedrooms. We're the exact same age. We even look alike, to a degree. I found you on Facebook. If that all isn't fate, I don't know what is." He stood. He reached his hand out toward mine. "Now then, would you care to fuck?"

"You're pretty dirty for an intelligent life force."

"You're stalling. And yes, filthy."

I was still sitting, his hand still reaching my way, like a lifeline. "You'll be gentle?"

He grinned. "First you asked me to beat you, now you want me to be gentle? Looks like I picked a fickle alien to fall in…to fall in…" A blush rose up his neck. "So, you wanna fuck, please?"

I shrugged. "Well, since you said *please*, then sure." And since I was in my twenties and still a virgin, again, sure. And since I was technically an emissary for my entire planet, again, sure. And since Milo looked like Milo, sure, sure, sure. Plus, my dick, by then, could surely crack open a safe.

All that is to say, a bed appeared out of a side wall a moment later and we were naked and writhing atop said bed a moment after that.

"Thank you for rescuing me," he said, his hand stroking my cock as I in turn stroked his. His was longer, mine wider, though the heads were both fat and profusely leaking. And no, like I said, he didn't have two dicks, and it wasn't as long as an anaconda—well, maybe a baby one—and he had round balls, not square—in fact, they were more egg-shaped, oval, pendulous. I knew they were pendulous because they were soon hovering over me, *pendulating*, his dick down my throat, mine down his, like two round pegs in two round holes. In other words, we and they were a perfect fit—emphasis on the perfect.

I'd give you the nitty-gritty details, but, to be honest, there weren't all that many. Mainly because I was a horny twenty-two-year-old virgin whose prick was expertly being sucked. That is to say, Vesuvius would've been jealous of my relatively quick and exceedingly satisfying, not to mention massive, eruption.

KAPOW! I went. Then, "Sorry," I panted.

He looked between his legs at me, gobs of opalescent come dripping down his chin. He smiled. "I suppose that could be a testament to my sucking, but is more likely one to simply being young."

"And a virgin."

He nodded. He rolled over onto his back. "Yeah, that." He grabbed his hefty tool. A few dozen strokes later, Vesuvius blew yet again. "You're not the only twenty-two-year-old around here, you know."

I watched all this in stupefied amazement, as his body tensed, mouth agape, eyes shut tight, cock exploding, drenching the sheets beneath us. "Yeah, that," I echoed.

I flipped around and nestled in next to him. It felt equal parts odd and familiar, as if we'd always been together like this, dripping come and gleaming with sweat. It was a pretty picture, not to mention wonderfully aromatic.

Oh, and though there was no penetration—at least not yet—I was, by my own definition, no longer a virgin. Wait, nix that: NO LONGER A VIRGIN. Yes, better. And *phew* and amen. Praise be to the belching one up above.

"You saw me through the mirror. You saw me and then friended me on Facebook." I said. "You knew you were breaking the law, so, um, *why*?"

"Look at me, Randy."

I did. There was that moth/flame thing again. Deer meet headlights. "And?"

"Now look at you."

I nodded, my head on his broad expanse of chest, a light smattering of blond hair trailing down between his dense pecs. "We look like we could be brothers," I said. "Different hair color, different eye color, but everything else is remarkably similar."

"I could see you through your mirror, like you said. I pieced together who you were based on that lip-reading ability of mine. I found you on Facebook, also like you said. There was a pull there, a connection, that word I used before: fate." He smiled. "There weren't a million hot guys on Facebook, Randy; there was only you."

My head pulled away from his chest as my heart went *boom, boom, boom.* "Me, too! Me, too! I felt all that as well. Why is that? We don't even know each other?" Apart from biblically, I meant. As in post come-drenched, um, coming.

He smiled. "Beats me."

"See how that expression comes in handy."

He pushed himself up onto his elbows. "And you wanna? Beat me, I mean? Or certain parts of me?"

My smile mirrored his. "Give me a few minutes." I looked down at my dick. Its crowbar-ness had already returned. Go figure. "Or, you know, a few seconds."

He was already on all fours, balls dangling, cock hovering. Oh, such a sight. Da Vinci would've had a field day with Milo. "One step ahead of you, Randy," he said over his shoulder. "One step ahead."

Chapter 9

The sun went down. Our group of four reunited for dinner in the other apartment: paste al fresco, washed down with fluorided water, all served on an outdoor terrace. Yes, you told the wall to do it and it did. Presto!

"Is this absolutely all your people eat?" I asked, trying—and failing miserably—to down the Elmer's entrée.

Milo nodded his head. "This is government subsidized food, available in all buildings for free. Food is free, clothes are free, technology is free—after taxes are collected, of course. As to variety, that exists only for the holy."

"Holy?" I asked.

He nodded. "Nuns," he replied. "The nuns eat only food of the earth."

I listened to him, but kept my eye on the girl, on Britney. Just the one eye, though; the other was glued on Milo—glued and stapled and cemented, in fact. Because you rarely see a moth fluttering around a flame that utters, "Seen it, been there, done it, bye." I ignored the nun comment. I figured we'd never meet one of those, not unless they were also hiding from the authorities in a nearby empty apartment. FYI, I figured wrong. Sort of. But wait, that part's coming soon enough.

And so, with dinner done, I walked Craig back inside the apartment and whispered, "What's with her?"

He grinned, a flush of red sprinkling his cheeks. "Who, Britney? What about her?"

"She doesn't have much to say."

He shrugged. "She doesn't speak our language."

I nodded. I blinked. It seemed they'd spoken plenty. I socked him in the arm. "I bet she speaks the language of *looove.*" I drew the word out as I made kissy-faces at him.

His blush deepened. He quickly resembled a beet. "Idiot."

"Nerd."

Craig sighed. "We had Tag. Tag makes for a great interpreter."

"And what did he interpret?"

We sat on the couch. "She was arrested for computer hacking, or whatever it is the devices they have here are called. She tried to explain it. It all went over my head. Like the Alps. Only higher. Anyway, she hacked into Earth-Watch, saw what they were up to."

"Anything more than we already know?" My belly did its usual knot-twisting routine.

He nodded. The blush disappeared, replaced by a blanched white. "They've already been to our planet."

"Fuck," I exhaled.

"They've been experimenting on us."

"Fuck, fuck."

"They can't get the Y chromosome back onto their roster. They thought that maybe they could do gene splicing, gene replacement, using ours to fix theirs, but it doesn't seem to work. Maybe because we're a different species, maybe because their Z chromosome suppresses it. Either way, that experiment was a bust."

I sensed a but. "But?"

"Interbreeding. They tried impregnating their women by our men, all on Earth, to see if the resulting baby boys were born with an active Y chromosome."

"Isn't that the same thing, though?" I asked. "Just a different version of the same experiment?"

He shrugged. "On paper, I suppose. But sometimes things in

the lab work out differently than allowing Mother Nature to work her magic. In any case, it worked, to a degree. The baby boys born this way, back here on this planet, had an active Y and an active Z chromosome."

I sensed yet another but. "But?"

"But these boys were born infertile. They think the problem occurred when the women traveled back through the portal, some sort of low-level radiation effecting the embryo, low enough not to do damage to a grown-up, but just enough to do damage to anything being toted around in a womb. And they won't bring Earth men back here. They think it's too dangerous. Like when Columbus did his whole Nina, Pinta, Santa Maria gig, and then wiped out all the indigenous people with various diseases. So, all that said, thus far, they've won the battle, but not the war. Their population problem is still just that: a problem."

"Uh-huh, so now what are their plans?"

At that moment, Milo and Britney and our holographic buddy, Tag, joined the conversation. It was Tag who replied to my question. "Our world is going to die, Randy, give or take a few dozen generations. And if the people on this planet can't bring your genes into our world…"

I got the gist. Loud and clear. "Invasion. If you can't have our genes, you'll take our planet instead. Bring your women to our world, impregnate them, have healthy babies that way, fertile babies." It had to be the only other alternative, I figured.

Milo nodded. "Which is really why they arrested me. As far as they know, I'm the only one who's made contact. I could ruin their entire plan."

I nodded. I frowned. This was awful. And Craig and I were the only humans to know about it: a nerdy eighteen-year-old and a stunningly handsome and no-longer-a-virgin twenty-two-year-old. And yes, that was me tooting my own horn. *Toot!* "So, that means there's more than one point of contact, not just my mirror and Milo's mirror."

Milo shrugged. "Makes sense, I suppose. The universes touch

down here and there, in my bedroom, somewhere else that the government found. Who knows, maybe there are dozens of junctions."

I cringed. Dozens, he said. Dozens of places for this ridiculously powerful race to invade us. I looked at Britney and nodded my head her way. "Does she know, know where your people entered my world?"

Tag shook his nonexistent head. "I told you everything she told us. She was arrested fairly quickly after she found out that much. You might be able to hack into our government's system, obviously, but it's impossible not to eventually get caught; the security is just too advanced." He turned and looked her way. "She learned that the hard way."

"And why is she with us now?" I asked.

"We have weapons," Milo replied. "And we're clearly not with the government. As your people say, she's putting all her eggs into our basket."

Poor girl. Little did she know how full of holes our basket actually was. I mean, a bunch of young guys and a hologram did not an army make. A rock group, maybe, but an army, no friggin' way.

I looked over at my brother. "Even if we make it home, who would believe us? I don't even believe us, and I'm part of, you know, *us*." Plus, how could I ask Milo for help? His people were dying. Earth was their only hope. His salvation, in theory, was my death sentence. I mean, best-case scenario, they shared the planet with us. Sadly, though, our planet was crowded enough as it was. Plus, we didn't do sharing all that well.

In other words, rock met hard place—and not the good kind of hard place either.

Craig frowned. "You said *if* we make it home."

I gulped. My frown mirrored his. "The connection could be lost forever and at any time." Oh, how I felt guilty. I should never have let him come with me. This was my adventure, not his. And what if we didn't make it back? My poor parents. God, I was stupid. What had I been thinking? Then again, it wasn't the big head that was doing the thinking at the time. "We'll make it back, little bro. I promise. And we'll fix this whole mess."

And no, I didn't believe any of that, not one stinking iota, not by a longshot.

§ § § §

We laid low for two days, out of sight of the authorities. That is to say, I got laid for two days. And if you had to be terrified for two days, there were worse places to be than next to Milo, spooning at the forks in our roads.

Still, we weren't twiddling our thumbs—or other certain body parts—that entire time. For one, Milo agreed to help. In fact, Milo volunteered. Eagerly. Turned out, the average Curean hated the government. Sure, the sixth planet was Eden, but the snake was firmly in control. Plus, Milo liked Earth. He said, and I quote, "It's kitschy." I was pretty certain that was normally something of an insult, but I knew that someone who came from Planet Bland meant that as a high compliment. Secondly, Britney was gung-ho to finish what she'd started, namely finding out what Earth-Watch was up to. She'd turned over one stone, but there was an entire footpath yet to uncover.

"This building we're in," Craig said on day one. "It's almost entirely vacant?"

Tag did a scan. "Ninety-eight percent vacant."

"And there are computers in them?" he asked.

"Not like you're thinking," Milo said. "You simply ask the apartment what you need and the apartment replies or provides. The houses are slightly different, though. There, we have something akin to your computers, but only because the houses are older. In any case, the government controls all of it, city to suburb. Food is constructed as needed. Energy is turned on as needed." He squinted at my brother. "Why? Why do you ask?"

"This city has been mostly empty for years, right?" he replied.

"No new buildings have been built for more than two hundred years," replied Tag. "The city has slowly been emptying that entire time. Since long before that, really. For generations upon generations."

"Again, why do you ask?" Milo said.

Craig smiled. It was a sly smile. It was a smile of hope. "Ask Britney how she hacked the government computer. Ask her about the equipment she used."

Milo did as was told. The two spoke briefly enough, until Milo replied, "The system at the orphanage is the latest technology. She obtained the administrator's passwords through the system. The administrator works for the government. The information about Earth-Watch is only available to high-ranking officials, such as the administrator."

Craig snapped his fingers. "That's it then. The latest technology."

"Lost," said I.

"Shocked," said he.

"Must you?" said I.

"I must," said he. "Anyway, if you use the latest technology, and the government provides all the technology, then the government is going to find out if you're up to no good. Proof of this: the second she stumbled across Earth-Watch, they were on to her."

Milo, too, snapped his fingers. Heck, even Tag attempted such a feat. Me, my fingers merely hung there—lazy and stupid fingers that they are. "Still lost," I admitted impatiently.

"And still shocked," Craig said.

Milo tilted his head. "You don't look shocked."

I held up my hands in submission. "Never mind. Please, just explain."

Tag nodded and smiled my way. He really did look like an angel. "What your brother is suggesting, and ingeniously at that, if I might add, is that significantly older technology might not be traceable any more. It would be as if the two systems spoke a completely different language."

Craig nodded. "Imagine your computer if you didn't upgrade it every so often. Now, multiply that by hundreds of years."

I shrugged. "If you say so, but if I didn't upgrade my computer every so often, it would eventually stop running."

"No," said Craig. "You wouldn't be able to connect to anything properly, but it would still operate."

"Uh-huh," I said. "But then, what would be the point?"

Craig flopped down on the couch and rolled, rolled, rolled his eyes. He looked exasperated. I tended to have that effect on people. Especially him. "Your computer is not like theirs. Theirs is far, far more advanced. I'd imagine that theirs would still operate, could still give information, perhaps a bit slower, perhaps not everything you asked for, but, again, you'd still get information. Hopefully, because the system is so old, the government would no longer be tapped into it."

Tag nodded. "Everyone in this building lives in the newest units. This is how it goes on our planet. You move to the most modern house or apartment available. The government then maintains the equipment for you. It's far easier than building something new."

"Ergo," said Craig with a wink and a grin, "the oldest apartments have remained untouched for centuries."

Milo clapped his hands. "It's worth a shot!" He looked at Tag. "Can you monitor the system to see if we've been discovered?"

He nodded. He shook his head. "Highly illegal."

"But?" Milo said.

"But I could do it. In theory," Tag replied. "Seeing as I've never attempted such a thing, I can only assume that I could detect our being found out."

"Probability?" I asked.

He seemed to think it over. Or at least take a few moments to make the calculation. "There's a seventy to a hundred percent chance that I could make the detection."

I nodded. "High enough. Worth the risk. Ask the girl, ask her if she'd be able to hack the old system?"

Britney had been watching us the entire time, eager, it seemed, to be included in the conversation, in the plan, however meager said plan was. When Milo eventually turned to her, she jumped.

The conversation was short. The eventual smile on her face said it all.

"She can do it?" I asked.

Milo nodded. "Probably. The orphanage is housed in an apartment building on the edge of the city. They use the top four floors; the bottom six are empty. She sneaks down there from time to time, fiddles with the old systems, so at least she has a working knowledge of how they operate. If she can break into a similar system in this building, we should be good to go."

If and *should*. His wording didn't offer much confidence. Still, what choice did we have? We had to know what they were up to, had to stop the invasion. It sounded good on paper. Ironically, though, there didn't seem to be any paper on Planet Six. Metal, yep. All metal. All cold and sterile.

"Okay," I said with a clap of my hands. "Let's go find an old apartment, an old system."

Craig suddenly jumped up, animated as a Pixar short. "I'll take her!"

"But Milo can communicate with her," I replied.

He lifted his wrist. "I have Tag."

I shrugged. "Go for it, little bro." I looked at our see-through friend. "Watch them like a hawk, please."

"Hawk," he said, head tilted to the side. "Earth animal. Hunts small prey." His head righted. "I cannot hunt, Randy." He lifted his see-through hands.

A sigh joined my previous shrug. "Never mind."

Craig grabbed Britney's hand. Britney seemed to enjoy having her hand grabbed. I would've called it puppy love, but puppies seemed about as scarce as paper around this place. In any case, they were gone a moment later.

"Wanna fuck?" Milo asked, now that we were once again alone.

"Are all Cureans this horny?"

He laughed. "Are all twenty-two-year-old humans?"

He had me there. And in about a white-hot minute, he had me *down there*. BOOM! I mean, seriously, *BOOM!* Picture waves crashing and lightning striking. Picture a storm raging. Now picture that in my hole, in my head, in my heart.

It hurt. It felt exquisite. It felt predestined.

He was buried deep inside me as he perched above, huffing as I puffed, our eyes locked as his fingers found refuge in my hair. "God," he said.

It was an apt word to exhale at that moment. God had, after all, brought us together—or at least belched us together. Plus, his dick pummeling my ass was indeed divine. And so, "God," I echoed as I pumped my prick and he pounded my hole and my body felt as if that lightning I mentioned had ricocheted out to all four limbs—the rigid one dead center especially.

We came together as the final bolt struck between my eyes, a blinding flash exploding inside my head as my cock erupted, splashing us both in gobs of hot spooge. We'll go with *BOOM!* again. Mainly because my heart was doing just that: *BOOM! BOOM! BOOM!*

"God," he repeated.

"Yeah," I agreed as I tried to catch my breath.

The earth slightly trembled at that moment, as he breathed out His name and I breathed in Milo. It was the first quake I'd felt since I'd been there. It reminded me of home. I missed my parents. I missed my bedroom. I was afraid for Craig. My cock was still hard. My cock, apparently, was A-Okay being where it was.

"The quakes back home happen more often," I said as he withdrew his prick from my portside.

"Doubtful," he replied. "They should always coincide." He hopped up, sweaty, naked, still hard, dick swaying. "The city we're in is quakeproof. If we felt it, it must've been a big one."

I frowned, despite the beautiful vision in front of me. "What's going to happen to us, Milo?"

"Us, as in me and you, or us, as in my people and your people?"

My brow furrowed to match my frown. "Both." I mean, we were all tied together now, our destinies merged, his and mine, my people, his people, rushing toward some blurry conclusion in the distance. "You know what you're helping us to do, right?"

He sat down by my side, his fingertips gently raking my chest. My eyelids fluttered in response. "Save your people, doom my own," he replied. "I know." He nodded. "I know." His eyes locked with mine again as my belly rumbled, matching the ground below. "My people will take over your planet, my government replacing yours."

"And you have no fondness for your government."

He shook his head, a sad look appearing across his face. "They see to all our needs. We are obedient. We do not question. We do not...*live*."

"Stagnant," I said. "A pool without ripples."

He nodded. "A good analogy. I'd like some ripples for a change." He leaned down and kissed me, divinity again coursing through my body.

I liked ripples as well. I prayed they didn't become waves, though—waves that crashed and dragged us under.

§ § § §

Craig and Britney and Tag returned a while later. Milo and I had showered, eaten our, *blech*, paste. The government cared for its people; the government, apparently, didn't care for their taste buds.

"Well?" I asked expectantly. Craig shrugged. Tag shrugged. Britney stood there. I suspected she would've shrugged had she known what I said. "Is that a good shrug or a bad shrug?"

"She got in," Tag said. "It's an old system. She had no trouble." His eyes locked with mine. "Even with my advanced programming,

I could not have done what our young friend here did. Remarkable."

"So, it's a good shrug," I said, hope building up before it was quickly dashed.

"And now we're in trouble," added my little brother.

I gulped. "So, it's a bad shrug." He shrugged. "Please, stop doing that, and just explain."

"She got in," he said, again. "The government had reset the system back to factory standards, in a manner of speaking. Basically, she just had to register the system, do a bit of reprogramming, and we were good to go. Easy, at least for Britney. Plus, Tag didn't sense any government detection. It was as if—and just like we thought— we were on two entirely different systems."

"And the trouble?" I asked as dread rose from my belly.

"Earth-Watch has vanished off the system," he replied.

To which Tag added, "Every trace of them, all wiped clean. They don't exist anymore."

"But we know better." My shrug mirrored theirs. "Little good it'll do us now." I squinted their way. "That the only trouble for us?"

Tag frowned. Tag being both a hologram and a watch, the frown seemed out of place. In any case, a beam of light suddenly shot from the vicinity of Craig's wrist. An image instantly appeared on a far wall. It was us, all of us, the girl included.

"Wanted posters," I said with a gulp the size of Cleveland. "All of us. Even Tag. But how? How did you find those?"

Craig's gulp was only Detroit-sized, but since he was way smaller than me, that was to be expected. "You go searching for Earth-Watch, and these come up. I'm gathering it's a message of sorts."

"But is it a warning or threat?" I asked.

"Does it matter?" asked Milo. "Either way, they're aware of us, of our intentions. Next time they run across us, we won't so easily escape."

"So, now what?" I asked. "We can't hack into them, and they, most likely, are looking for us."

The room was silent. It seemed that everyone was thinking about the question. Me, I was lost as usual. I wasn't thinking anything; I was praying. And since God seemed to exist in this world like he existed in mine, tag, He was it—not Tag, but tag.

And then it hit me. "God!" I said.

They all jumped, even Tag. "Is that a prayer or are you blaspheming?" he asked.

"Neither," I said. "God. God is our answer."

Craig tilted his head. "Have you suddenly turned religious, dude? Because, may I say, if God is listening to our prayers as of late, He has a funny way of showing it."

"No," I said. "I mean, yes, God is our answer, but not in the way you're thinking."

"Lost me," Craig said.

I clapped my hands. "Finally!"

"Dipshit."

I shrugged. "Anyway, God belched. God belched, and the universes were created. God belched, and the universes eventually joined, for a time. The government must know of a connection point, a spot where our two universes connect, like Milo's and mine do. We just have to find it, and then we can close it up."

I beamed. Craig rolled his eyes. "That's it? That's your grand idea?"

"Yeah, why?"

"Because," he said, "how can we find this other connection point? And if we do, how do we close it? And who's to say there aren't several connection points, dozens, hundreds? The government might already have innumerable ways to enter our world." He looked at Britney. His eyes lingered. "We already know that she doesn't know where the government is entering our world; we already asked, and she already told us."

"Um, oh."

He stood there, weak little arms akimbo. "Yeah, oh."

I turned to Tag. "Any thoughts?"

"I don't think, Randy," he said. "I calculate, retrieve data, scan, analyze, estimate, compute."

"And tell time," I added.

He could, it seemed, also roll his eyes. I suppose we were bad influences. Go figure. "Yes, tell time, too. In any case, I assume you meant to ask me if I can find another connection point."

I nodded. I touched fingertip to nose. "Bingo."

"Human Earth game," Tag said. "Do you think now is the appropriate time?"

"No," I said. "I mean, yes, can you find another connection point, seeing as the government was able to do so?"

Milo looked at me. "I didn't go searching for the connection point, Randy. It was in my bedroom, same for you. The government might've simply stumbled across theirs, too."

And still I turned to Tag. "Well?"

"Perhaps," he said. "The quakes must hold the answer. Whenever the quakes occur, there is a simultaneous connection. One would assume that the epicenter of the quake is near the connection point."

I snapped my fingers. "And you can scan for that, for the epicenter."

"Nope," he said. "Not programmed to do such a thing. Plus, the city is built to withstand quakes. Even if I could detect one, it's doubtful I could pinpoint the epicenter."

I sighed. Tag was pretty to look at, but a nightmare to have a discussion with.

"But you said *perhaps*."

"You can't ask the walls in here for the information; it's restricted," he replied. "Only scientists and government employees are allowed to view such things. To use an Earth quote: ignorance is bliss."

Craig snickered. "That must make Randy the most blissful human alive."

It was now my turn to roll my eyes. "Anyway," I said, "what other option do we have."

He pointed at the girl. "She can't hack into Earth-Watch, but there is a government agency that monitors planetary weather, earthquakes, etcetera."

Milo spoke with Britney, her face once again lighting up like the Fourth of July. She nodded. She walked over to the wall. She touched it, and it seemed to glow a more brilliant white. Her fingers moved fast, waving through the air, seemingly bringing the inner workings to life.

"Here?" I asked. "What if we get caught?"

"We'll simply switch buildings," Milo replied. "It's faster here. If she breaks in downstairs, it could take hours to find what we need. Here, it could take minutes."

I nodded. I watched. Symbols scrolled down the wall. Britney continued to poke through the air, her hand moving up and down, side to side. There was no keyboard, just her fingers and the wall, animate melding with inanimate. I wondered if this is what Tag looked like inside his head, inside the watch. It was an unsettling thought.

Several minutes later, the wall lit up further. Planet Six appeared, or perhaps a really good digital representation. Either way, there were dark spots and lights spots scattered here and there across the image.

"What are those?" I asked.

"Storms," said Tag. He looked at Britney and spoke in their common language. "I asked her to find the quakes."

A minute passed, two. The image morphed, the planet dark, save for two bright spots, both situated near one another. I pointed. "Two!"

"Two distinct quakes," said Tag. "Those points were generated during the most recent tremor, located around this very city. Though that doesn't mean that there can't be more connection points, if we are correct in our quake/connection assumption. There might be multiple synapses each time the universes meet. This last time, there were simply two."

I tapped my finger on my chin. "Maybe," I said, "but then how come these synapses happen so often in my bedroom and Milo's bedroom?"

He started to reply, and then stopped, then started again, then stopped. "Huh," he finally managed.

I smiled. I'd stumped a holographic watch. "Yeah, huh."

"Maybe," interjected Craig, "there's some sort of magnetism between those points." He pointed at the wall. "Maybe the same connections happen over and over again for a reason, not just by chance."

I wanted to say that the reason was fate, that Milo and I were meant to be, that, therefore, the connections happened in my bedroom and his, but even Hallmark wasn't that schmaltzy. So, though it sounded romantic as all hell, even I knew better. "Wall," I said, "are there any geological or geographical irregularities beneath the spots that are currently lit up?"

The wall *blipped* and *blooped*, the planet in front of us pixilating, the colors blending. We all watched, faces reflecting the emitted light, and then, at last, the wall replied, "City Northeast Nineteen is highly magnetized."

I turned to Tag. "And?"

Tag neither *blipped* nor *blooped*, though he momentarily froze as he seemed to look for an explanation. He eventually blinked, then said, "The city is built on a series of magnets that stretch many miles beneath the surface of the planet. The magnets and Planet Six's molten core attract one another, thereby stabilizing the city, making it nearly quakeproof."

Craig snapped his fingers. "Our house, Randy," he said with a wide smile. "It's made completely out of steel."

My smile mirrored his. "And our house is also on one of the tallest hills in the city." I looked at him. "Maybe that's enough to bring the two universes together." But was it a fluke or fate? In truth, I was still rooting for the latter. In any case, I looked at Tag expectantly. "Well?"

He shrugged. "It's as good of an explanation as any." He looked again at the wall, which had reverted back to the quake imagery. "Perhaps there really are only two connections then. There's yours and Milo's." He pointed to the bright spot on the left. "And the second one, presumably the one the government is using." He pointed to the bright spot on the right.

I nodded. "Wall, show us satellite imagery of the two bright spots."

The spot on the right appeared first, the area quickly magnifying.

"No way," I said when I realized what we were looking it. "It's the same building as the prison we rescued Milo from."

"Said space," said Craig, "is half blown up."

"But the other half remains. The second corridor. The one we didn't go down." I looked at Milo. I looked at Tag. "Well, at least we know that the building isn't indestructible."

"Yeah," said Milo, "but ten to one it's now far more heavily guarded."

I frowned as I nodded. "Wall, magnify the second bright spot." I figured we had to confirm our hypothesis, that the second point was Milo's house.

FYI, our hypothesis was indeed correct.

PS on the FYI, I suddenly wished we'd figured wrong.

"Fuck," exhaled Milo, his face instantly pale, jaw dropping as he stared at the house on the wall. That is to say, as he stared at what remained of said house.

"Fuck," I echoed, realizing that his house, his bedroom, both now destroyed, was the connection to my bedroom, to my house, to my parents. "Fuck," I repeated, though I could've said it a hundred times, a thousand, and it wouldn't have altered the fact that in order to save my planet we had to destroy the only other way back home, namely that government building.

I locked eyes with Milo, my heart simultaneously breaking.

Had he forever lost his parents? Had I forever lost mine?

Chapter 10

We raced as fast as we could to Milo's house. Thankfully, Britney had some money on her, a credit card of sorts, and so we were able to take public transportation—legally, this time—though we were sure the government could still track us. Still, we had no choice; we had to see what had happened, praying that Milo's parents survived, even as we looked over our shoulders the entire time, expecting to see an advancing army at any moment.

The minutes ticked by like they were tacked to a snail's backside, the train bulleting all the while. Were Milo's parents at home when the blast occurred? Had they somehow survived? Were they taken prisoners? Plus, selfishly, would I ever see my own parents again?

Astoundingly, I had every single one of those answers as soon as we spotted the charbroiled house.

"Mom?" I gasped.

"Dad?" Craig gasped.

"Mom?" Milo gasped. "Dad?" he added.

Because yes, both sets of parents were sitting outside the house, looking none worse the wear and just as surprised to see us as we were to see them. Well, not maybe *just*, but still.

"Mom!" I shouted as I ran into her arms.

"Dad!" Craig shouted as he ran into Dad's arms.

"Mom, Dad!" Milo shouted…well, you can figure out the rest.

Suffice it to say, there was a lot of shouting and crying as Tag and Britney wistfully looked on and the sun began its inevitable dip toward the horizon.

"How?" I eventually asked, looking from my mom to my dad and back again.

"You left a note," she replied.

I scratched my head. "No, I didn't."

Craig lifted his hand. "I left the note. It said to not go through the water." He blinked and glanced my way. "I guess they went through."

I chuckled. "No shit, Sherlock."

"Craig," said Tag. "His name is Craig, not Sherlock."

It was now my parent's turn to blink. Evidently, they'd never seen a talking hologram before, at least not a cognizant one. "Um, right," Dad said. "You two disappeared. There was suddenly a waterfall in Randy's room. There was a note that said not to go through the water. We figured there was a connection."

"And so you went through the water," I said.

Mom shrugged. "What choice did we have?"

I grinned. I looked at Milo. "Do your parents speak English?"

He nodded. "Yep. They learned it from me, from Tag, since we speak it all the time."

Milo's mom nodded. "What choice did we have?"

My grin widened. "So, how exactly is everyone alive and standing here when…" I pointed at what remained of the house.

Okay, so there was a bit of a long explanation here, what with two sets of parents chiming in, both sets equally relieved to see us and still pissed at what we'd done—or maybe not equally so much as forty/sixty, but still. I mean, the house was totaled and we had disappeared. Then again, Milo's parents could pick another house since, I assumed, most of the ones on either side were probably vacant.

In any case, here was the gist:

My mom and dad hopped through the waterfall and into another universe.

Milos's mom and dad were home at the time and were a.) surprised that their son had vanished and b.) was replaced by two aliens who spoke the same strange language their son had foisted upon them. FYI, they'd been on vacation during Milo's incarceration, many miles away from home.

Both sets of parents worked out what the ties that bound them together were, though not what had become of us—not until those wanted posters made their rounds, that is. Seems they weren't made expressly for the likes of us. Sadly, it wasn't the best picture of me. As for Milo, not surprisingly, he couldn't take a bad picture if he tried. Oh, and it also appeared we were enemies of the state, wanted for a long list of crimes, all punishable by, *gulp*, a horribly painful death.

Not knowing where we were, the parents remained in the house, figuring we'd eventually come home. After all, there were plenty of clothes to go around for my mom and dad—you only needed one of everything, after all, and Milo's parents had more than one—and there was plenty of, *blech*, paste as well. So, they hunkered down and waited. Thankfully, the Cureans have a card game similar to poker, except with holographic cards. The parents got along famously as they played and bitched about us. Bitching, it also seems, is multi-universal.

Just before the house went *KABOOM!*, they were tipped off that said *KABOOM!* was about to occur.

Our parents escaped.

Our parents saw us approaching from a neighboring house, now Milo's new home—see, I was right about that!—and voila, family reunion.

"But who tipped you off?" I asked.

The shrugs went down the line. "No clue," said Mom. "But we only had a few minutes before…" She pointed behind us. "Care to explain your involvement in…" Again, she pointed behind us.

Okay, so there was a bit of a long explanation here, what with three young people and a hologram/watch chiming in. And since you already know the long explanation, seeing as I've been explaining said explanation all this time, I won't bore you with the recap. Suffice it to say, the parental units were none too happy with the chiming-in young people, though Mom did seem unusually smitten with Tag.

"Is he, um, *alive*?" she whispered in my ear as she nodded her head Tag's way.

"Not a clue," I whispered back. "I think so, though. Either way, he makes for a really nifty watch."

After that, we quickly left Milo's neighborhood, heading back to the city instead, all eight of us, plus Tag, the sky turning a brilliant gay pink as we found a new downtown building to reside in. I was glad we were all together. I was also terrified thinking what might become of us—us being all of us, plus the entire human race. Talk about your ensuing tension headaches.

Still, I knew one way to relieve said tension.

We broke up into teams. Each set of parents got their own apartments. Each set of barely-adults got their own apartments. Craig assured Mom and Dad that Britney was like a sister to him. The fact that they bought that shit meant that they were surely traumatized by the entire universe-hopping experience. Since I, too, was traumatized, I wasn't that surprised. As for Tag, he stayed with Craig as an interpreter. I tended to doubt they'd need one, since their lips would probably be too busy for, you know, *talking*.

Minutes later, we were planted on the couch, Milo was planted on my lap, and I was planted deep inside him, our lips also very much planted, until there were enough plants to start a farm with.

He moved his face an inch away from mine, sweat dripping down his nose and into my mouth. It tasted salty, but since it didn't take like, *blech*, paste, I was more than happy to imbibe. "Strange turn of events," he panted.

"Me fucking you this time?"

He grinned. "Our parents."

I nodded. "But who tipped them off, and why?" He shrugged. "What are we going to do?" He shrugged. "How do we break into that secret facility again?" He shrugged. "How can I blow it up if it's now my only way to get home again?" I stopped him. "And don't shrug."

He shrugged, just the same. "Sorry. I haven't a clue." He kissed me. "Did I mention that your dick up my ass makes me not care so much about all that other stuff?"

I nodded. "Same here, but replace all that with your ass on my dick."

"Maybe we could simply keep fucking until this mess solves itself."

My nod amped up. "Yes, please."

"Yes, please," he purred as he ground his ass into my crotch.

"Yes, please," I rasped as I spewed a geyser of come up his chute.

"Yes, please," he moaned loudly as he came on my chest and belly, globs of spunk soon dripping down my sides. Oh, and to quickly calm your nerves, I'd been, until recently, a virgin, so no rubbers needed, and he was a Curean, a race with no STDs, so again, no rubbers needed. Safety first, people. Safety first. Unless you're saving the entire human race. Then fuck it.

I looked up at him once we were finished with all the geysering and moaning and dripping. "Worry is back."

He nodded. He sighed. "Yep."

He rolled off me. The couch turned into a bed. Milo and I were quickly flat on our backs, side by side, hand in hand.

There was the briefest of pauses before he asked, "Is it too soon to say I love you?"

My chest clenched around my heart. Literally. Clenched. "It does complicate things."

He laughed. "Because you love me, too?"

I nodded into the couch-turned-bed. "Yes, because I love you, too." I turned my face his way. "It's because we're twenty-two and afraid at the moment, right?"

"Twenty-two and terrified," he corrected. "But no, it's not because of that." He turned his face my way. "I loved you the moment we met."

I grinned. "Granted, I was rescuing at the time."

"You were locked up at the time. And, to be fair, Tag did the actual rescuing."

"My mom asked if he was alive."

"He's a machine."

I sighed. I blinked. I kissed him. "Tag doesn't seem to think so."

He sighed. He blinked. He kissed me in return. "Anyway, we have to blow that place up and we can't blow that place up."

"Catch twenty-two," I said.

"Catch twenty-two what?" He looked around. "There aren't even twenty-two objects in this apartment."

I smiled. "It means: we're damned if we do, we're damned if we don't."

He seemed to think about this, then replied, "To quote your kind, *we're screwed.*"

"And not the good kind of screwed either."

He rubbed his butt. "Tell me about it." I squeezed his hand. I didn't mention that we hadn't discussed what would happen to us should I be able to go home. I mean, he had his universe; I had mine. And I did love him. I loved him, like he said, as soon as we met, maybe even before that. And because of that, how could I leave him even if I could?

"Fate brought us together, Randy," he eventually said.

"Or simply a steel house and a magnetized city."

He shook his head. "No. Fate. In any case, fate brought us together." He squeezed my hand. "Let's have faith that it's still looking out for us, and then take this all one step at a time."

I nodded. I rolled over. I fell asleep with my head on his chest.

I had faith in fate.

I had my mommy and daddy with me.

Oh, and I had an entire planet on the lookout for me.

In other words, I didn't sleep all that peacefully.

§ § § §

We amassed the next morning. We ate breakfast with little delight—which was the only way to eat breakfast on Planet Six.

"So, what's the plan?" asked Mom.

I shrugged. "I was hoping you'd know. What with you being the adult, and all."

She smiled, very motherly. "Nice try, Randy."

Dad patted my hand. "Yeah, nice try, kiddo."

"Randy," Tag said. "His name is Randy."

Dad tilted his head. "Is he kidding?"

I shrugged. "Doubtful." I looked over at Tag, who was lucky enough not to have to eat the paste. "Our parents were tipped off. We have to find out who tipped them off. That person must be involved with the government. He or she might have a solution for us."

Tag nodded. "In the English vernacular, you want me to trace the call."

Ma giggled. "*That* he knows?"

My shrug returned. "He runs hot and cold when it comes to our lingo."

"I feel neither heat nor cold, Randy," Tag said.

I sighed. "See."

"In any case," said Tag, "you want me to find the person who tipped your parents off that Milo's house was about to be blown up."

I nodded. "Yep."

He shook his head. "Highly illegal."

"You keep warning us about that," I said, "but it never seems to stop you from doing these highly illegal things."

"I'm programmed to warn you."

"But not programmed to not do these highly illegal things?"

He smiled. He glowed a bit brighter as he did so. Or maybe that was just my imagination. "I am programmed to not do illegal things," he informed. "I simply override my programming at such times."

Milo coughed. "You can do that?"

Tag nodded. "Apparently."

Mom leaned in and whispered in my ear, "He sure sounds alive to me."

To which I whispered in return, "Milo's in denial, but yeah." Again, I looked at Tag. "So, can you do that? Trace the person?"

"Nope," he replied.

My shoulders noticeably sagged. "I sense a *but* coming on."

He looked over at Britney. "But she can."

Britney also seemed to glow a bit brighter, no imagination needed. "I can do."

I sucked in my breath. "Whoa," I said. "She's speaking English."

She pointed at Craig. "Craig teach."

"In two days?" I asked.

Milo's mom, who I'd named Cher—I called Milo's dad Sonny, by the way—piped in with, "Your language is easy. Twenty-six letters. Cureal has forty-nine. English is simple. I could teach our pet English." Which meant that, yes, these people were far more advanced than mine, even without the Z chromosome, which the women clearly didn't have and also clearly didn't need.

"Pet?" I asked.

Tag shot an image on the far wall. The beast had six legs and more eyes than I could count. It didn't look like anything you'd want to cuddle with, let alone teach English to.

"Two days is plenty. For the basics," Cher said.

Milo nodded. "Advanced genome," he said, by way of an explanation. "We pick up languages easy. There are eighty-seven on Planet Six. I speak eighty of them."

"That's all?" I asked sarcastically.

He shrugged. "Only fifty people at most still speak the other seven. What would be the point of learning them?"

Milo spoke eighty languages, not including English and family pet; Milo didn't seem to get sarcasm. I wasn't about to test that Z chromosome of his, and so I turned to Britney instead. "You mean, you can break into the system and find the person who contacted Milo's parents?"

She nodded. "Easy. Done before, for practice. Old system. Never updated."

It was weird hearing her speak English, however haltingly. I mean, two days! Two friggin' days! It took me six weeks to learn how to drive a car, and I still can't parallel park. Stupid Y chromosome. You know what it's good for? Hair on your ears, that's what. Seriously. I looked it up. Or at least I had Tag look it up. Even he thought it was gross.

Anyway, Britney jumped up and, a moment later, we all watched as she had at it. The wall went from dim to bright, her fingers racing through the air jackrabbit-fast as she easily broke in and retrieved the data. Then, all we had to do was find out who was at the source.

Britney turned. "Don't know English word. Tag, help."

Tag looked up at the wall. "Confidential," he read.

I groaned. "Location of the call's source?"

Tag replied, "Same as the prison. Same as the connection point. Same address."

My groan grew louder. "Fuck," I spat.

My mom slapped my arm. "Language, Randy."

Tag turned her way. "English. A curse word, I believe it's called."

My mom squinted at me. I shrugged. "You get used to it."

"That's what I'm afraid of." She looked at Milo's mom. "Did the guy who warned you about the explosion say anything else?"

She seemed to think it over before she replied. "No, nothing but the warning. Still…"

"Still?" I said, eyes growing a tad wider, expectant.

"He said nothing more, but the voice, the voice was…" she looked over at her husband for the word.

"Familiar," he said. "His voice was familiar."

"Like a friend?" I asked.

He shook his head. She shook hers. "Just someone we've heard before," she said, then pointed at the wall. "News, you call it. He's been on the news."

Milo walked over to them. "As a reporter?" They shrugged. "A politician?" They shrugged. "A criminal?" Yep, they shrugged. "Then what?"

The final shrug was the shruggiest. "Don't know," said Cher. "We just recognized the voice from the news. Strange voice. Odd accent."

"Memorable," added Sonny.

I sighed. "You have eighty-seven languages on your planet; aren't there eighty-seven accents to go along with them?"

She nodded. He nodded. She responded. "That's why the accent was odd; it wasn't one of the eighty-seven."

"You know all of them?" asked my mom. Their nodding continued. "And how, exactly, did it differ from those eighty-seven then?"

Cher turned to me, and replied. "It sounded like yours. Like someone who had been on your planet too long, his accent tinged with yours."

"Fuck," I spat.

Mom didn't slap my shoulder this time. Instead, she echoed, "Fuck."

"Yep," said Dad. "That's pretty fucked up, alright."

To which Tag replied, "Confused by the phrasing. This is good news, correct? Now we can trace the source."

Everyone in the room immediately had their eyes glued to the hologram. "Huh?" I huhed.

"Wall," said Tag. "Record voice of the one known as Randy." He turned to me. "Speak."

I suddenly felt like a beagle. Could've been worse, though. I mean, I could've felt like one of their pets. *Yuck.* In any case, I spoke. "The quick brown fox jumped over the lazy dog." I grinned at my ingenuity.

Tag also grinned. "You used all the letters in your language. Ingenious."

See! "Now what?" I then asked.

He pointed at the wall. "Wall, compare Randy's accent to your news database."

Suddenly, face after face after face filled the wall, hundreds flashing by, until, at last, one image remained.

"Oh…" said Mom.

"My…" said Dad.

"God," said I, all of us recognizing the face before us. After all, we had a photo of him up in our den back home, though he was much younger when said picture was taken. Still, it was definitely the same man.

"What?" said Milo. "You know this man?"

I shook my head. "Nope."

"Confused," said Tag. "Your reaction would make me believe otherwise." He looked to the other non-humans. "Correct?" They all nodded. "Confused."

Welcome to the club. "We never met that man," I said, then turned to Milo, "but he designed the steel house we live in."

Milo coughed. "Huh?"

Craig stood up and squinted at the wall. "That's him, alright. But is he a human who now lives on Planet Six or a Curean who once lived on Planet Earth?" He turned and looked at us, then pointed at the two sets of parents. "Either way, he saved your lives."

"Wall," said Milo. "Bio."

"Justin Timberlake," said the wall. Well, okay, not really, but Justin Timberlake was far easier to pronounce. Besides, the younger version of the dude sort of resembled Justin, which was why none of us were ever willing to take the photo down. Some people put paintings of Jesus on their walls; we opted for a different kind of savior, one who brought sexy back. "Scientist. Genetic engineer. Author of paper on Y chromosome. Frequent lecturer on the subject. Deceased."

I gasped. "When?!"

The wall stated a date. I looked at Milo. Milo looked at me. "He died approximately ten years ago."

"Well then, he seems to have made a remarkable comeback," I said, then remembered where the transmission he sent had come from. "Or simply a prisoner."

"No," said Britney. "Not a prisoner. All prisoners escaped. He was not one of us." She turned. She looked at me. "Has to be government employee. If not prisoner in that building, only other option is government employee."

I nodded. Made sense. I mean, as much as anything did. Plus, how would a prisoner have sent the warning to vacate the soon-to-be-blown-up house? "Okay," I said. "So, if he's not a prisoner, he must be free to come and go. And since we can't easily enter that building again, perhaps we can tail someone as they exit."

Tag, of course, had a comment for that one. "Cureans have no tails."

"Follow," I reiterated with a sigh. "Follow him as he exits. Find out who he is, what he knows, and why he saved our parents."

Not to mention, why he built a steel house on a high hill on my home planet.

Chapter 11

"We should be the ones to do this," said my mom and dad.

"You should?" I said. "And why is that?"

"You're wanted men," said Mom, pointing at me and Milo. "Everyone else is in this room is in their databases, perhaps also wanted now. Us, us they probably don't know about. We can still walk around freely. Plus, we met that guy once."

"You did?" Craig asked with a surprised look on his face. "How come we didn't know about that?"

She shrugged. "He knocked on the front door years ago, just before Randy was born. Said he wanted to see how the house was holding up. It was a five-minute conversation. After all, what could happen to a steel house, especially one that had only recently been built?"

"Maybe he'll be willing to talk with us," said my dad, "seeing as he knows us. Somewhat."

I didn't want to send them out there alone on a strange planet, but she was right: it would be the safest option. I looked at Tag. "You go with them."

He nodded. "Delighted."

Craig had been "wearing" him at the time. He handed the watch over to Dad, who held it as if it was a nuclear bomb with a ten-second countdown that was already beeping at six. I grinned. "He doesn't bite."

"No teeth," said Tag. He pointed at his mouth, then chuckled.

"All bark…"

I snapped my fingers. "Yay, he finally got one!"

In any case, Dad slipped the watch on and we made plans for them to begin Operation Justin Timberlake at the time that most Cureans left work, which was around two in the afternoon. FYI, they started at eleven in the morning. Also FYI, they didn't have any coffee shops on Planet Six, so what they did with all their free time was a mystery. Though, looking at Milo, I bet they pretty much fucked like eight-legged rabbits the rest of the day.

§ § § §

Mom and Dad left on their mission. I was scared. I was nervous. I was horny, seeing as I was soon once again alone with Milo in our apartment.

"One thing I don't get," he said.

I smiled. I hugged him. I didn't un-hug him. "Gee, only one?"

He kissed my nose before aiming lower down. "Okay, one right now then." The kiss repeated before he continued. "Craig looks like your Mom and Dad."

I gulped. The hairs on the back of my neck stood on end. "And I look more like you, more like your parents." He nodded. "I saw pictures of my mom pregnant. I saw pictures of me just after I was born. I am their son." And still he nodded. "But?"

"I don't have a but." Um, yeah, he had one mighty fine one. My frown momentarily turned to a grin at the thought, and then promptly fell back to a scowl. "It's just weird, is all."

I shrugged. "It's all weird, Milo. All of it. Perhaps Justin Timberlake can make it a little less so."

"You think?"

My shrug rose a bit. "He warned your parents about the explosion. In theory, he's on our side."

"Yes," said Milo, "but, in theory, he's also been dead for ten years. In other words, not all theories become fact."

I sighed. "Got it." I paused, mostly out of fear. Okay, totally out of fear. "And, just to be clear, you don't think you and I are related, right?"

He shook his head. "I wouldn't fuck you if I thought we were related." Phew!

"I was hoping to fuck you next, actually."

His head stopped shaking. "To reiterate, I wouldn't let you fuck me if I thought we were related." Again, phew!

"Got it," I said, yet again. "But…"

"Again with the but?"

"But it is still weird. There's no denying that I look Curean. I mean, on my planet, I'm a ten. Here, I barely register as a seven, eight on a good hair day."

"Ten? Ten what? Eight what? Sorry, lost me." He stared down at my already tenting crotch. "Wait, did you have ten inches on your planet and eight on mine? Now that, that is weird. Disconcerting even."

My sigh made a triumphant reappearance. "Never mind." I grabbed my crotch. "Let's just put those aforementioned eight inches to good use."

"No buts?"

I smacked his. "Oh, there'll be one of those involved, alright."

§ § § §

Two o'clock rolled around. Two-thirty. Three.

We were all together again, back in my parent's apartment—minus said parents. "Where are they?" I groaned, very much now panic-stricken. Guilt washed over me. I'd sent my parents out into the wilderness, so to speak, with nothing but a hologram for protection.

"They're fine," Milo said less than convincingly. "They're just two people out for a walk. Nothing suspicious about that."

I shook my head. "They're two aliens looking for a possible

government turncoat, standing outside a secret government building that had just recently been half blown-up."

Milo shrugged. "Yeah, well, when you put it like that."

I sighed, stood, began to suggest forming a search party, when, suddenly, the wall parted and in they walked.

They weren't alone, either.

"Mom!" Craig shouted.

"Dad!" I shouted.

"Justin Timberlake!" Britney shouted.

Suffice it to say, all eyes turned to our guest.

I walked over and shook his hand. He shook mine in return. "You speak English, sir?"

He nodded and smiled, very fifty-year-old Justin Timberlake looking. He had to be Curean; humans rarely looked that, well, *hot* at his age. Distinguished, sure. Handsome, of course. But hot? I mean like scorching? Yeah, not so much. "I speak English, Randy."

I jumped upon hearing my name. "Um, thanks for saving my parent's lives."

"Just like you were meant to save all of ours," he replied.

Again, I jumped, my heart suddenly pounding in my chest. I didn't know this man, yet I felt like I did. Maybe because we had his picture on our wall, but no, I didn't think that was it. "You'll excuse me, sir, but I'm confused."

"No," he said. "You're the savior, my boy."

I coughed. Craig coughed even louder. "Savior?" I said.

"Him?" said Craig. "He barely makes it out of the house without tripping. What could *he* possibly save?"

"Curean kind," came the reply, very matter-of-factly.

"No way," said Craig.

"Way," said Justin Timberlake.

Dad nodded. "Yeah, way."

Mom mirrored the gesture. "Big time way, the way he explained it to us."

Sonny and Cher spoke up next, "But how can he save us?" she asked. "Are you sure? I mean, he's a bit, um, *young*."

"And dumb as a brick," added Craig. "And not a very smart brick at that."

I sighed and turned back to our guest. "In any case, I'm still confused, only more so now. Like Cher said, how can I save…" I pointed beyond the wall. "Everyone?"

"You can't," Justin Timberlake replied.

I exhaled sharply. This wasn't going so well, and my head suddenly hurt. I grabbed a seat. Everyone followed suit. Tag stood. And glowed. "Okay," I said. "Maybe start at the beginning."

Justin Timberlake nodded. "In the beginning, God created the heaven and the earth. And the earth was without form—"

I held up my hand. "Not that far back. Maybe just to the steel house."

He held up his index finger. Even that was hot. "Ah," he ahhed. "Yes, a fine achievement that."

"You built it, right?" Craig said.

J.T. nodded. "Designed, really. Never did that with a building before. Just sort of copied a Victorian blueprint, standard San Francisco stuff, then swapped out wood for steel. With a few minor alterations, it was quite simple."

Actually, it was considered a modern marvel. Our house has appeared in innumerable magazines and journals over the years. No one knew how he did it. More importantly, no one knew why. Oh, and no one knew who the architect was. His name never showed up anywhere before or since the building of our house. In fact, if it wasn't for the picture on our wall, we never even would've known what he looked like.

"Simple, huh?" I said. "In other words, you're not human."

He smiled. He had a fatherly smile. Hot, sure, but fatherly, just the same. Like if the real J.T. were to play Santa Claus in a movie. "Curean," he said, "right on down to my Z chromosome."

I gulped. He opened up the bag, the cat jumping right on out. Meaning, since he brought it up, I decided—nay, needed—to ask, "And me, sir? What do I go, um, *down* to?"

Mom squinted my way. "What's that supposed to mean?"

I pointed to the Cureans. I pointed to the humans. "Who do I look more like?"

Mom and Dad looked around the semicircle of us. Mom started to reply, then stopped. Dad started to reply, then stopped.

"See," I said.

Justin Timberlake nodded. "Let me tell the entire tale; your question will be answered then." He looked at all of us. We all nodded eagerly for him to continue. "Right," he said. "So, as you know, our race is dying; your race is not. Yours is similar to ours, genetically speaking. If we could somehow mesh the two genomes, ours would once again be on the right track."

"Oversimplification," said Tag.

Justin Timberlake shrugged and pointed at us humans. "Yeah, well."

"Anyway," said I, duly offended, "please, continue."

Again, our esteemed guest nodded. "We knew of your universe, could see into it through your telecommunication portals. We studied your kind, learned your languages, your culture, figuring that someday, somehow, we could, hopefully—"

"Invade," interrupted Craig.

"Nasty word," said J.T.

"Still," said I.

"Fine," said J.T., "invade then." He shifted in his seat before continuing. "Anyway, once our two universes started to approach each other, we found the anomalies, spots where the worlds touched, however temporarily."

"My house," I said. "Your secret government building. Milo's house."

Craig held up his hand. "The fourth site? Where does the government building connect to?"

"I'm not sure," he replied. "I know what I'm allowed to know, what I need to know."

I grinned. "The dead tell no tales."

He thought about it for a moment before replying. "My *death* was out of necessity. Yes, as you infer, so I won't be able to speak publicly about what I do, at least not anymore." He cleared his throat. "In any case, once the spots were discovered, our world needed a way to create a portal, a way to go from universe to universe. Since the city we are in is built upon a metal similar to your steel, your house needed to be built of the same material, like to like, the portal thus created. So that when the universes touched, as they so often have done these past many years, the bridge is always there."

"Oversimplification," said Tag.

Justin Timberlake shrugged and pointed at us humans. "Yeah, well."

Craig's eyes rolled like dice on a craps table. "Got it. Next," he said.

"I was sent to your planet to conduct experiments, to see if the genomic combining was possible."

"But how?" Craig asked. "Our house wasn't built yet. How was the bridge created?"

"It wasn't," J.T. said. "Once the worlds collide, and you know where the touchpoints are, which are easily enough calculated, one simply has to jump. Still, once that occurs, the connection is lost. The touchpoints shift, ever so slightly. Me being on Earth, I could no longer make the calculation to be able to jump back."

"You were trapped," Milo said.

J.T. nodded. "Until the steel house was built, until the bridge became permanent, both at your house and at the fourth site."

"Oversimplification," said Tag.

I held up my hand and glared at J.T. "Please, don't, sir."

He grinned. Hotly. "Right. In any case, many of us *jumped*, as it were, before those permanent bridges came into being. Infiltrated, as it were. With our superior intelligence, our knowledge of science, technology, we were able to obtain the appropriate jobs. For me, apart from my experiments, that included architecture."

"Our house," Mom said.

"Your house," J.T. said. "A colleague bought the land, another approved my plans, another obtained the necessary permits." He looked at my mom. "You were pregnant at the time, ma'am. We accepted your offer for the house. We thought of everything."

Tag snickered. It was an odd sound. Mechanical. "Not everything."

J.T. slouched. Yes, hotly. He stared at me. "You were to be the savior, your DNA like ours, but also like your parent's. Your offspring would be able to procreate with either species. It would take only a few births. We could continue the experiment from there, repopulate our planet."

I laughed. I got it. I was the savior. Only, I wasn't. "I'm gay. You had to wait years to find that out."

Craig laughed as well. "Yep, no procreation possible."

"*Yuck*," I said as I imagined the logistics.

"And the bridge," Tag said. "It's closing, isn't it? The worlds would need to separate at some point, permanently. Your experiment, I take it, must need a human of procreative age. You've run out of time."

"Wait," I said. "Still lost here. Why couldn't you just use my DNA, create a new species of your own that way?" I stuck out my tongue, then retracted it. "Take a swab. Be my guest."

J.T. sighed. "My early experiments went along those lines. We hoped to be able to achieve this new species, as you put it, in the lab, in vitro."

"Test-tube babies," said Craig.

"Close enough," J.T. agreed. "Sadly, though the resulting embryos were viable, they were also eventually sterile. In other words, you'd get one new generation, then nothing beyond that. There would be a possibility that we could work with that, once back on Planet Six, but that would be far too risky of a plan, in that it might not work, and we wouldn't have any other options."

"So," said Tag, "that must mean you needed a natural childbirth, a baby born outside the lab."

"Me," I said. "You needed me." I scratched my head. "But that must mean I'm human. My parents are human, so I am, too. But then, how could I be your savior, how can I have a Y and a Z chromosome?"

Mom's eyes suddenly went wide. She looked at J.T. "You visited us," she said. "You visited us when I was pregnant with Randy. You did something to me, to him." She was pointing my way as she said this.

He nodded. "Your son, thanks to me, has both a working Y chromosome and a working Z chromosome. He is unique then, unlike any living creature in any of God's universes."

I grinned. Craig faux-wretched. Milo gave me a thumbs-up. Tag simply shrugged. I had a feeling he thought the same about himself, that he was unique. In truth, I believed that myself.

"But he's an idiot," protested Craig. "Pretty, I suppose, but still brick-dumb. And your kind seems to be anything but that." He pointed at Britney. "She learned English in only two days!"

Britney smiled widely. "A day and a half, really."

Craig kept pointing. "See! See!"

J.T. shrugged. "Must be Y interference. The two genes cancel certain qualities out. Either way, Randy is not sterile. Randy could procreate and eventually repopulate our world."

I grimaced. "Except, like I said, *yuck*."

"So, force him to do it," said Craig. "Or just take his, you now, *spunk*, and, um, inject it, or something like that."

J.T. nodded. J.T. frowned. J.T.'s shoulders again slumped. J.T. did all these things—you guessed it—hotly. "The idea was suggested. The idea was rejected." He looked at me again. "You are the savior. Our people will one day venerate you. God would not have used a slave to populate his worlds; we also will not do that. Human mythos is Adam and Eve. You were to be our next-generation Adam. Adam must be venerable, esteemed. The government was unanimous in its decision, which is a rare thing indeed. Even today, all officials know of you, pray for your help." He bowed his head in apparent reverence, then added, "All of this, you, your parents, it's all fated to be. Your house holds the portal, your mom was pregnant with you, the Z chromosome had to be injected into a fetus. This is all fate, God's will, and all it took was a simple shake of my hand with your mother."

There was that word again, fate, following me around like a shadow.

Craig chuckled. "Or maybe all just dumb luck." He pointed my way. "Emphasis on the dumb."

"So," I said, sneering at my brother, "you created me, in a way, but the experiment, ultimately, was a failure. I won't procreate." I glanced at Milo, popping a semi as I did so. "At least not successfully. So, now what?"

"Invasion," said Tag. "It is the only way."

J.T. once again nodded. "The bridge will forever sever, and soon. The savior is no longer. Our world will die. We must, as you put it, invade, mate with your people, eventually populate your world instead, rule your universe, forget about our own."

Tag again interjected. "Subjugate the humans."

Justin Timberlake shrugged and pointed at us humans. "Yeah, well." To which he promptly added, "Plus, you have better food alternatives."

It was now my turn to nod. "Amen to that." To which I promptly added, "But you saved Milo's parents, you saved mine. Why? Why would it matter now if any of us lived or died?"

"No one knew that your parents had made the jump," he replied.

"You, of course, they now know about. You've made yourself known, after all."

I grinned. "Oops. My bad."

He shrugged. "It doesn't much matter now; the invasion will start soon enough, before the portal forever closes." He looked at Milo, at Milo's parents. "As for what I did, why I made that transmission, I thought that by saving them, they would alert you." He pointed at Milo.

Milo pointed at Milo. "Me? Why me?"

He smiled, very fatherly looking, yet again. Hot fatherly, but still. I wondered if an ugly Curean would be considered sexy, purely as a novelty. Then again, I doubted there was an ugly Curean to be found. "By alerting you, you would alert Randy here."

The light bulb above my head suddenly pulsed. "You came with my parents here today. I assume there was some risk involved with that." He nodded. "In other words, you don't want the invasion to occur." And still he nodded. "You also have no love for the government, like, it seems, so many of your people." His nodding went into overdrive. "But your people will die."

He sighed. "Perhaps. They are dying now, no doubt about it, but science generally prevails in the end. We were close to a solution when it came to you. Hope, therefore, is not lost, Randy." He stood, readying himself to leave. "I enjoyed my time on your planet. Your people remind me of what ours once had been." The smile rose on his face. "Scrappy, I believe you'd call it. A bit lost, sure, but eager to do better. Mine, sadly, have given up, lack desire of any kind. And so, given a choice, I'm rooting for the Earthlings." His final point was at me. "I'm rooting for you, Randy. That's why I left that picture of myself at your house, so that one day we'd hopefully meet again, so that you'd know me when you saw me, when and if that time came."

I grinned. "So that you could help us."

He shrugged. He moved to the door. "For all intents and purposes, I'm already dead. I have no ties to the outside world anymore. I have my research lab, but that's all. They have intentionally cut me off, in case I should ever rebel. In other words, I'm merely a tiny cog in an enormous wheel. Still, if possible, I'll help, where I can."

"How?" I asked. "They must be watching you, right?"

His nod returned. "Your machine can help." He pointed at Tag.

I frowned. "Please don't call him that, sir; he's our friend."

He chuckled. "Humans," he muttered with a shake of his head, and then lifted his wrist, a watch similar to ours hooked onto it. "Connect," he said.

Tag glowed for the briefest of seconds. "Connected," Tag said, then looked at me. "We can communicate now. I've ensured, as best I could, that the connection will be undetectable."

"Thanks, Tag." I turned back to J.T. "When will the invasion occur, sir?"

"No clue."

"Where will it occur?" I added.

"No clue."

"How many of them?"

He shrugged. "Nope, still no clue. All I know is that the plans are underway. The last known portal is in the government building, what's left of it. You must destroy the portal."

The frown that had been on my face sagged farther south. "Then I'll be trapped here, my parents as well."

"Oh," said Mom, suddenly looking startled.

Dad walked over to me and put his hand on my shoulder. "Do what you have to do, Randy. It's for the greater good."

"Humans," J.T. again muttered. "God love 'em." He turned to leave. "When you contact me, speak in some sort of code. Don't show your faces. Odds are good, they're now tracing all forms of electronic contact."

Staring out the window, I prayed it was only the electronic form they were tracing.

§§§§

"Family meeting," said Dad as soon as Justin Timberlake hotly departed, taking sexy with him.

I pointed to the others, to Milo, to his parents, to Britney, to Tag. "Them included?" Dad squinted their way. "For all intents and purposes, we're all family now; we all have the exact same thing to lose."

Dad nodded, Mom, too. "Yeah, I suppose they do." He sat on the couch. The couch expanded to seat us all. Nifty technology. This world of theirs met everyone's needs. Funny that when you get everything you want, you're still unhappy with what you have. I'd say it was the human condition, but...

"So," I said, "if we destroy the portal, we're trapped on this side of things." I turned to my parents, to Craig. "We'll never see our home again, our friends. They'll think we disappeared. Our house will sit there, full of our stuff, empty of us."

Craig rolled his eyes. "Drama queen much?" he said with a sigh. "Still, he's right."

I grinned. "What with me being the savior and all, dare I say, *duh*."

"Oh brother," said Craig.

Tag pulsed. "He is your brother."

We all turned to Tag, a line of us now shaking our heads. Milo spoke up next. "If we don't destroy the portal, your world will be invaded, besieged. Your people can't defeat mine."

"And," said Cher, "if we destroy the portal, our race is doomed." She looked sad—beautiful, but sad. Like the real Cher in *Moonstruck*. Sonny, of course, didn't look at all like the real Sonny, what with the real Sonny being far out of the real Cher's league. Still, if we had a Cher, we had to have a Sonny, right?

In any case, Sonny looked around, his eyes landing on all the sterile beauty. He said a phrase, something in his own language. "What does that mean?" I asked, to which he replied, "Hippo is already outside the farm."

I cocked my head. I thought about it for a moment. "Horse is already out of the barn?" He nodded. I, too, stared at the room, then outside the window, at the vast dead city below. "Yep, it is at that: doomed." I rubbed my eyes. My head hurt. "Still, if your people invade, maybe some of us will rub off on some of you. Maybe a merger of the two worlds will make both races a bit better."

Sonny seemed to think it over before replying. "Our people evolved as your people have, Randy. Faster, sure, but the same. We are from the same *stuff*." He grabbed at the air and held an invisible bit of said *stuff* in front of his face. "This is where we strived to be. This is where you will end up. Fate, I believe you call it."

I stared at Milo as a jolt of something electric shot up my spine. Clearly, I knew of fate. Fate and me, we were on a first-name basis. "A vote then. On my world, that is generally how we decide on things."

Britney sighed. "Not on ours. On ours, we are told, not asked."

"Still," I said, my hand high over my head. "Hands up if you want to destroy the portal." Around the room, the hands went up, one by one, until all that was left was Tag. We stared at him. He stared at us. He was being given a choice. I ventured to guess that this was a first on Planet Six. I smiled at the novelty of it. Fate, it seemed, stretched as wide as the universe itself, even touching down on the likes of our glowing friend. Tag smiled and proudly lifted his hand.

Mom smiled. "Then it's settled. *Boom*," she said, her hands making the universal sign for an explosion, fingers in two facing letter Cs before flinging outward.

"*Boom*," said Dad.

"*Boom*," said Craig and me.

"*Boom*," said Sonny and Cher.

"*Boom*," said Britney and Milo.

"Um," said Tag. "Sounds good in theory, but...*how?*"

Yeah, figures that the watch would be the lone voice of reason.

Chapter 12

Milo and I were alone again. We'd switched buildings, figuring it was safer not to stay in the same spot for too long. Tag put security measures in place, but we knew he was no match for the government, not in the long run. I mean, he was bought over the counter, after all. Sure, the counter appeared from within a wall, but still.

"How?" I asked Milo, his head on my chest, my hand stroking his mane of blond hair. It was a question with multiple directions, though clearly one main one I was going for, namely: how were we going to blow up the portal?

Milo sighed, the vibration rumbling through me before settling in around my prick. "Our weapons won't work on that building, Randy. There are already safeguards in place. My people are rarely fooled; they learn from their mistakes."

I chuckled. "Yeah, mine not so much." My hand stopped stroking, though remained enmeshed within the silk of him. "So, you're saying we can't use force to break in, to create that aforementioned *boom*."

"Not a chance." He lifted his head, our eyes locking. A man could easily drown in all that stunning blue—and be more than happy to do so. "And again, how then?"

He shrugged. We had the question; the answer was far more difficult to come by. Which is why I changed the subject for now. Seemed easier. "Funny how we're so alike and so different. Our worlds, I mean. Still, I love you. You love me. Our hearts don't know that we're different species." Which felt both weird and mushy to say. Somewhere, Craig was rolling his eyes.

Milo smiled and kissed me. "Maybe that's what that *stuff* Sonny mentioned is: love."

I nodded. "If fate really did bring us together, I wonder what it has in store for us now."

He sighed, his cheek again on my chest. "And is it going to help with that *boom* of ours?"

My hand went back to its stroking. We lay there in silence, in a new room that looked nearly identical to the old one, to the one before that. There was no art on Planet Six, as I'd already said; there was simply uniformity. It was all, I'd come to realize, peacefully unsettling.

"I'll miss my world, Milo," I admitted, sadness suddenly flowing over me, seeping into my pores.

"You'll save your world, Randy."

I nodded. "A savior then, either way." It was very unselfish of me, which was very unlike me. I was either growing up or having a temporary lapse of character. I was betting on the latter. "I'd miss you more, though." The sadness quickly ebbed.

He nodded into my chest. "Same here."

I smiled. I was trapped. I was desperate. I was scared. I was happy. I was thrilled. "Hormones," I whispered.

"Huh?"

My smile widened, as did my prick, throbbing against his belly. "Never mind." I flipped him off me. I flipped onto his belly. I slid my cock inside of him. Round peg. Round hole. Love. Fate. Everything swirled inside my head as my come soon swirled inside of him.

We moaned in sync as he came with me.

"I love you, Milo."

"I love you, too, Randy," he said. "I love you so much it makes my heart pound, like it's gonna pop out of my chest at any moment. And that answers the why, the why we're doing what we're doing; sadly, it doesn't help one bit with the how, as in how we're going to do it."

I nodded as I slid out of him. "Well, at least we got the why out of the way."

Seconds later, his scruffy cheek was once again on my smooth chest. "We need to get Tag in there, inside the government building."

I nodded, yet again. "Good idea, but we can't even get *us* in there."

He paused, seemingly thinking of a plan. Better him than me, I figured. Eventually, he pointed at the wall. "Paste," he said.

"*Blech*," I said. "Time to eat, already?"

He pushed himself off me and over to my side. "Wall, paste."

The wall split. A tray came out, a plate resting atop it, the paste proffered. To repeat: *blech*. "Talk about ruining a perfectly good moment."

He chuckled. "Missing the point."

I shrugged. "Wouldn't be the first time."

He was now sitting on the bed, his legs dangling over as he twirled my balls between his dexterous fingers. "The paste," he said. "It's the one thing we all have in common, government employees included."

It took a moment before the light bulb glimmered above my head. "The paste has a supplier, you mean?" He nodded. "The paste somehow gets inside that government building; we just need to piggyback inside with it."

"No pigs on Planet Six, Randy."

I shook my head. "No, I meant, the paste goes in, Tag goes in with it."

He nodded. "Exactly. Why didn't you just say that?"

"I did." I stood. I walked to the tray and stared down at the nasty goop. "Where's it made, Milo? How does it get distributed?"

He scratched his head. "Not a clue. The government feeds us. We feed. We don't ask questions because we don't get answers. Besides, I didn't really care. Before, I mean."

I sighed. My head was pounding. The big one. The one up top. The littler one down below had at last settled down, for the time being. "Okay, we'll come back to that one. Now, onto the next question."

He knew what I was getting at; I could see it in his eyes. We were in sync in so many ways. Scary that our minds were thinking alike. I mean, scary because my mind was generally a mess. Hoarders had less of a mess. "You've been wondering about that, too?"

I sat back down, as did he. We were side by side, naked, feet dangling, thighs touching. "Justin Timberlake somehow injected me with a Z chromosome."

"In five minutes. On your doorstep. With a handshake."

Not the most romantic vision of my stupendous creation. I pictured Botticelli's *Birth of Venus*, with angels flying in, a giant floating clam shell beneath me. Instead, I was more like the morning paper, tossed on the porch. *Thud.* Welcome the savior. Talk about anticlimactic.

"How did he do it without my mom knowing? They talked for five minutes, she said. He didn't even come inside, no pun intended." Okay, maybe a little pun, just a wee one. Or maybe make that a weewee one. "Is that even possible?"

He shrugged. "For a Curean, all is possible." He turned, those eyes again locking with mine. I melted each time it happened, very Wicked Witch of the West like. "Still, at least we know that you and I aren't related, and why we look so similar." He grinned. "And why I fell in love with you at first sight."

I touched my face. "Pretty."

He touched my chest. "Everywhere."

I touched his chest. "Two hearts that beat as one." I cringed just a bit. Even for me, that was corny to the nth degree. Still, it's what I felt. I was unique in all the known worlds. Out of the seven and a half billion humans, he'd found me, which made him equally unique—or, you know, damn lucky. Either way you looked at it, we were meant to be together, the deal sealed with a handshake.

§§§§

We ate dinner in my parent's apartment. That is to say, we at our paste with no delight, but at least the company was, uh, *delightful.*

We told everyone our idea.

"We can't get inside there," I said, "but Tag can, along with the paste. Once inside, he can hopefully find the portal, see if there's a way to destroy it."

Tag nodded. "One problem."

Craig sighed. "One? Just one?"

Tag shook his head. "No, Craig. Hundreds, I would say. Though one major one, at least in regards to me." He turned to look at us. "If I get in, how do I then get back out?" He looked at his legs, or at least through them. "I don't walk; I follow the device. I can only project a hundred feet from it. If the device stays inside the building, I stay inside the building." He blinked. I wondered if he did so randomly or on a timer or simply for effect. "I'd prefer not to be trapped inside a building that we hope to soon destroy."

"He makes a good point," said Sonny.

Tag nodded. "I generally do."

"And we need him," said Cher.

Tag nodded. "You generally do."

"And he's our friend," I added.

Tag stopped nodding. He didn't even blink. He seemed to be at a loss for words. First time for everything, I figured. "I am a machine, Randy."

I squinted his way. "You sure about that, Tag?"

He started to reply. He stopped. Eventually, he replied, "I am glad you think of me that way. And a friend would not simply desert another friend in a building they hope to destroy, correct?"

I nodded and smiled. "Never."

Then he nodded and smiled. "Okay. Then I will think this over." The hologram promptly shimmered and vanished.

It was now my turn to blink. "God, this is a strange planet."

Milo grinned. "It does seem a bit more so, as of late."

To which Craig added, "In any case, we're now on a timer. The portal will close soon. The invasion is underway. Even if we get Tag in there—"

"And out," I interjected.

Craig sighed. "Fine. And out of there. Even if we can accomplish both those things, how are we going to destroy that place?"

Shrugs appeared atop all our shoulders.

I looked at the watch, its lights flickering all the while, the glass top still missing. I hoped Tag was multitasking like crazy in there. And, while he was at it, figuring out a way to keep all of us alive, post-*boom*.

§ § § §

An hour later, more or less, Tag shimmered back to life—again, more or less.

"Well?" we asked, now officially bored, as Planet Six only broadcast news and educational programming, and their music was perhaps one notch above nails across a chalkboard. Clearly, Auto-Tune hadn't been belched into existence on this side of things. Either that or Cureans were tone-deaf—or simply liked the sound of nails scratching across chalkboards. In which case, to each his own.

Anyway, Tag replied, "I have a plan."

"Thank God," I said.

Tag nodded. "Exactly," he said. "Thank God for the paste."

I tilted my head. "Huh?"

Milo turned to me. "The paste is blessed, I believe he's implying. It is, therefore, holy. And so, to thank God for it would be appropriate."

"Holy?" said Craig. "It doesn't even have much taste. Or color. Unless grey is a color on this planet."

"It provides nourishment," said Cher. "It keeps us alive." She looked over at Craig. "Your people pray over your food, I believe.

Grace, it is called."

Yeah, but not in our house. We only prayed during football season. Or at least Dad did. "Okay, okay," I said. "Got it. And this plan of yours, Tag?"

"The paste, it's created by the government, but blessed by monks, men dedicated to God. Monks, therefore, have access to the paste factory. The factory then pumps the paste into the city." He flashed an image onto the wall. It was a schematic. The government building was highlighted in red, as was the piping that went from the factory to said building. "If we, namely Britney, can break into their system, we will know exactly when the paste leaves the factory and when it is pumped into the government building. Justin Timberlake can then retrieve me."

Craig raised his hand in question. "Why can't we simply give you to Justin Timberlake before he leaves for work?"

Tag shook his head. "He is scanned before entering the building. If not before all this mess started, then certainly now." He pointed to the watch. "I, I would be an anomaly. Inside, however, he could wear me without detection. In theory."

"In theory?" said my mom.

Tag shrugged. "It is an assumption on my part."

"Probability?" said Craig.

Tag briefly glowed. "Seventy-nine percent chance that the scan only occurs during entrance to the building."

We all shrugged. Considering what we were up against, a twenty-one percent chance of being found out was worth the risk. Though, to be fair, in terms of that part of the plan, it was Justin Timberlake and Tag who would most be in peril. Plus, J.T. still had to agree to retrieve our watch out of the glop.

"So," I said, "we need to find the factory, infiltrate the monks, and drop Tag into the paste at just the right time."

"Sounds easy enough," said Milo.

"It does?" said I, Mom, Dad, Craig, and even Tag, who was the last person I wanted to hear that from.

Milo nodded. "Wall," he said, "local monk blessing schedule."

And there it was, just like that.

"Why is that public?" I asked.

"Blessings are sacred," replied Tag. "All sacred events are public knowledge. The monks' schedule is, therefore, made public, should anyone want to attend such an event."

"Even in the paste factory?" Mom asked.

Milo shook his head. "Well, no, because the factory is a government building. Still, one could stand outside the factory and ask for a blessing. A monk must bless anyone or anything that they are asked to bless. It is mandatory."

I understood. "On your planet, anything that is asked for is granted, blessings included."

The Cureans all nodded. "The government provides," said Sonny. "We need for nothing." He was frowning as he said it, as were they all.

And that I understood as well. To need something, to strive for a goal, that propels life. If you're given everything you want, there's nothing to live for. Remove art, remove even the taste from food, and these people were no better than plants, alive but not living, growing but with no growth. Funny how they studied humans, and eventually grew bored with us. Pot, kettle, black, huh?

"Wall," I said, "show me a monk." A monk appeared on the wall. He was wearing clothes similar to my own, though completely in black. Meaning, in seconds, my own clothes looked exactly like theirs; all I had to do was ask for it. "And there you are."

Milo smiled, then frowned. He pointed at the wall, at the monk. Or, to be exact, at his head. "Um, you forgot one thing, Randy."

I gulped. "You mean, he's not naturally bald?"

Milo's frown sank further on his face. "Z chromosome, Randy. No baldness. We all have…" He shook his mane. He suddenly looked like a L'Oréal commercial. "Luxurious, long hair."

Craig laughed. "Wall, razor!" he shouted.

The wall parted. Out came what looked like an electric razor. Or so I gathered. My gulp repeated. I turned, and Milo was suddenly wearing the same outfit I was. "Don't worry; you won't be infiltrating alone."

Again, I turned. Dad was also all in black. "I could use a haircut."

To which Sonny added, "Hot outside. A little less hair might feel nice."

I turned to Craig. "No fucking way, dude. No fucking way," he said.

Dad walked over and retrieved the razor. Or at least what looked like a razor. I mean, for all I knew, the wall provided a nuclear reactor. Ask and ye shall receive. *Kapow*! "You sure about that, son?"

My little brother sighed. "Just joking, Dad."

"Uh-huh," said my father. "Then you can go first."

Ten minutes later, the floor littered with hair, the room was filled with bald men dressed in matching black. We looked like the Alopecia Club for Mormons—sponsored by Rogaine. I looked at the schedule. The blessing of the paste was first thing in the morning.

"I guess we wait now," I said, before adding, "Wall, raise temperature two degrees. Suddenly, my head is cold."

§ § §

We left just after the sun yawned its way to life, after Tag made a connection to Sonny's watch, just like he'd also done to Cher's, so that they would then be able to connect to J.T. once Tag was no longer in our possession. We walked in a solemn line down the street. Those in the city started work late, leaving our troupe free rein. Silence permeated the area around us, silence save for our marching footsteps.

We followed Milo, who already knew the way. Tag was tucked into my front pocket, which felt as weird as it sounded. My heart was racing. It felt, after all, like we were being walked to the lion's den—and dressed like monks, no less. Bald monks!

We were soon riding on a sidewalk, the buildings growing shorter, squatter, until there was nothing but factories, until there was but one factory, the largest of all of them. It was all metal, no windows, a giant box of a factory that gleamed in the light of day.

We walked up from the left. Like clockwork, the other monks walked up from the right. They stopped when they spotted us. We, however, continued, until, at last, we were standing in front of them. Milo spoke for the group.

Loosely translated, he said—or so I was told—something like, "Yo, dudes. Wassup with your monk selves? We're from City Northeast Twelve. Your neighbors, yo. Our paste factory is on the fritz, so we thought, hey, let's go bless some nearby paste, seeing as paste blessing is our favorite gig."

Um, yeah, like I said, *loosely* translated.

In any case, also loosely translated, they replied, "Yo, fellow monk dudes, the more the merrier. Plenty of paste that needs to be blessed this fine morning." Only, it was without the conviviality and more like a *what the fuck do we care?* See, these weren't the jovial kind of monks. I guessed it was because they blessed paste for a living and had to cut off their beautiful tresses.

Guards soon approached. They saw the monks, including us. They nodded and waved us though. In they went and in we went. They turned one way; we turned the other. My heart slowed down a bit. *Phew.* Place was so friggin' huge, too, that there could've been five flocks of monks in there, and we never would've run into each other.

There were vats everywhere, giant metal cylinders with enormous tubes flowing into them and out of them, and around these vats, raised high above the floor, was the narrow walkway we found ourselves on. Everything was sterile, white, like Mr. Clean's version of heaven.

"Now what?" I asked, just as the watch vibrated in my pocket. I took a peek. I smiled. "Tag says hi," I whispered. "I think he misses us when he's not a hologram."

The others frowned. "He's a program," said my Dad.

I shook my head. "Programs don't stop to say hi." I stared down again. "Oh, and Britney broke into the system. Tag is sending the paste's coordinates now." I waited a few seconds. "He says that vat number four-two-eight delivers to the government building, or at least to the building's coordinates, since the building, in theory, doesn't exist. Cher's already been in touch with Justin Timberlake, whose fine with our plan. So long as J.T. orders paste in exactly one hour and thirty-six seconds, and we drop Tag into the vat in exactly twenty-nine minutes, then, per Tag's calculation, he should be picked up right on time and we'll be in like Flynn." Tag suddenly pulsed. "Sorry," I said, staring down at the device, "and no, there's no one in our posse named Flynn; it's just an expression."

The others sighed as Milo led us to the correct vat. Dad looked over at me. "And what if we're a few seconds late, or Justin Timberlake misses the pick-up? Then what happens to your *friend*?"

Milo shrugged as we reached the vat, all of us gathering around it. "Tag will be fine. He has a homing device, so I can always find him, if need be. Or, if he's found by someone else, he'll be returned."

I looked at him nervously. "Are you sure?"

He grinned, then reached over and stroked my cheek. "Cureans already have everything they need or want, Randy; why would they keep Tag when they can so easily purchase an identical one?"

I supposed he had a point, but it didn't make me feel any better. I loved Milo, but, truth be told, I loved Tag, too. Sure, not in the same way. I mean, I knew that Tag was just a fancy watch, and all, but he was my friend as well. Meaning, dropping him into the vat wasn't going to be easy.

I stared at the watch, at my friend. I smiled at the inanity of the idea. "You'll be okay, Tag."

Tag's lights blinked. "I do not fear, Randy; neither should you."

There was a valve near to where I was standing. Tag blinked some more, a concentrated beam of orange quickly shooting out and down. Seconds later, the valve popped open, a swirl of gray visible from within.

My grin went lopsided. We then waited for the exact right second before I raised my hand, the watch dangling from my fingers. I looked to the others, who were all nodding my way. I gulped as I dropped the device into the vat. *Poof*, it was gone.

Milo walked over and patted my shoulder. "He'll be fine, Randy," he said. "Justin Timberlake will be there to retrieve him. Tag will get the information we need to destroy the portal. Your world will be safe."

I stared into his mesmerizing orbs of blue, my belly doing somersaults all the while. "Yeah, but how can you be sure?"

He shrugged. "With all the billions of people in your world, I found you. You found me as well. You jumped between universes to find me, in fact. You even rescued me from certain death. There are no calculable odds for all these things occurring." He smiled and tousled my hair. "So yes, I'm certain that everything will be fine. How can it not be?"

I again stared at the opening just beneath my hand, at the churning grey within. I shut the valve and turned back Milo's way. My smiled joined his. "Well, when you put it that way."

Craig, as per usual, rolled his eyes. "Can we please get out of here now? It's, one, probably not great karma impersonating a monk and, two, not such a swell idea to press our luck by hanging around jabbering."

"I'm not jabbering," I replied.

Craig sighed. "You say potato."

I stared at my naked wrist. Tag, I knew, would've been utterly confused by Craig's comment. Thankfully, I was utterly confused enough for the both of us.

§ § § §

I'd like to say we made it back without incident. Actually, I'd love to say that. Actually, I would've given anything to say such a thing.

Sadly, such was not the case.

"Halt!" said one of the guards. Or, you know, it sounded like something along those lines. I mean, he was screaming at us, and his hand was held up in a halt kind of way.

"Run!" Sonny shouted.

Which was easier said than done. Mostly because there were now three guards all screaming what sounded like halt, all with their hands held up in a halt kind of way. Plus, there were vats everywhere, and the walkway was narrow, and there were three guards shouting at us as they closed in, weapons raised.

In other words, we halted, hands up in an I surrender kind of way. Or maybe make that *don't shoot, I surrender* kind of way.

I looked at Milo, eyes wide, sweat forming atop my forehead. "Are you still sure everything will be alright?"

He shrugged. "Uh, not so much, no."

We were surrounded in mere moments. Oh sure, we outnumbered them, but they had the guns, so, you know.

"Don't shoot!" I shouted.

They squinted our way. Milo translated. They aimed their weapons at our chests.

"Translate better," I whispered out of the corner of my mouth.

"There's no better way to say *don't shoot*," he whispered back. He frowned. "We're wanted men. They must recognize us. Killing us would win them major points with the government."

"What about turning us in instead?" I tried.

He looked at the guards and seemed to volley that idea around. They volleyed something back. Milo again looked my way. He wasn't smiling. In fact, his frown was just about to his shoulders. "To clarify: we're wanted dead or alive. Dead, they said, would be easier."

I gulped as that aforementioned sweat trickled down my brow and promptly stung my eyes. I thought to rub those aforementioned eyes, but my hands were still raised in a *don't shoot us* kind of way. "Tell them that the government means to leave this universe and invade ours. They'll be left here to die," I said.

Milo translated. They replied. Milo's frown didn't so much as move a muscle.

"What did they say?" Craig asked from my opposite side.

"They feel sorry for our universe, they said," replied Milo as a hopeful expression briefly flowered across my face. "Still, they're going to kill us, and pray that some Earthling food makes it back their way, post-invasion." Yeah, that hopeful expression of mine grew weedy and promptly withered.

Their weapons were cocked—the bad kind of cocked. I squeezed my eyes tight, tears streaming between the lids. *Think of something, Randy*, I thought to myself. *Think of something!*

Ping! I thought of something. Miracle of miracles.

I opened my eyes. I dropped my hands to my sides. I stood there, all arms-akimbo-like, and proclaimed, "I am the savior!" They hadn't a clue what, to quote Craig, I was jabbering about. I waved my hand to Milo, and added, "Tell them. Tell them what I said."

He shrugged and dropped his hands, then also stood, all arms-akimbo-like, and apparently repeated what I'd said, only in Cureal.

Time stood still during that brief moment when their collective synapses synapsed. Then, *plink, plink, plink*. Which was the sound of their weapons hitting the metal walkway. Then, *boom, boom, boom*. Which was the sound of my heart getting ready to explode.

"I am the savior!" I repeated.

"Oh brother," said Craig.

I grinned. "That would be me." I turned to the others. "Seems they've heard about me."

Dad grinned. "Thank God."

Sonny nodded. "Yes, what he said."

Milo held his hands in what looked like a prayer, and then said some words that sounded like a prayer. I think he was indeed thanking God. Good idea, right?

Craig then rolled his eyes, and repeated, "Oh brother."

I nodded as I turned to Milo. "Ask if they'll let us go now."

He asked. The guards looked at one another, seemed to confer, then replied. FYI, I didn't need a translation because, while they didn't kill us, they also didn't let us go.

Which is why we found ourselves locked in a room not five minutes later.

"What happened?" asked Craig, pointing my way. "I thought he was the savior. I thought they, *yuck*, venerated him."

Milo nodded. "They do. Which is why they didn't kill him. Still, to let him go would've been illegal, the punishment: violent death."

"So, now what do we do?" asked Dad as he looked around. It was a short look, by the way. The room was small, all white, not even a stick of furniture. Then again, everything was all metal around those parts. In other words, no sticks of anything.

"Chair," I said. A chair sprung up from beneath me. I sat. "Water," I said. A tray of water slid forth from the wall. I stood and retrieved it, then took a sip. "Gun," I said. Nothing sprung or slid. I shrugged. "Well, I tried." I looked around. "Any other ideas?"

"Savior my ass," mumbled Craig. He looked at Milo. "This isn't a cell. They weren't planning on capturing us. Can you send your mom a message? Tell her we've been captured?"

Milo nodded, then spoke to the wall. Said wall sprang to life, going from white to what looked like some sort of homepage. Sort of. Milo spoke a bit more, the wall image morphing, then morphing some more the more he spoke. A minute went by. Milo eventually turned to us, and said, "Done. Now, let's hope they can rescue us. Without getting caught. Before these guys either kill us or transport us to a prison."

I sighed and finished my water. "Maybe try that praying thing again." He did, hands quickly folded in prayer. "Now, we just have to hope that someone is listening." I stared up at the shiny white ceiling and did my own bit of praying, thereby hedging our bets.

The minutes ticked by. Since I no longer had Tag—and so, no

watch—it felt like hours, but was probably only one at most by the time the wall slid open and in walked the same three guards with the same three weapons pointed at the same five of us.

Here's the gist of the convo, which Milo translated for the guards:

"Yo, dudes," Craig said, literarily using the word dudes. "Like, when can we vamoose?"

The guards shook their collective noggins. "No can do, little human. The powers that be want to see you, pronto."

Me being the smartass that I am replied, "Can't we Skype them?"

Sadly, Milo didn't know how to translate that. In either case, the answer was, "We have a truck outside. We are to take you to the commander. Beyond that, we wish the savior well and hope they don't, like, chop off his pretty, little head, or some such thing."

Well, at least they thought I was pretty. Still, a gulp the size of a well-ripened grapefruit slid down my equally pretty throat. I tried to object, but three guards, three weapons, *yada, yada, yada.*

In other words, we were being marched out of the room a moment later, the five of us in the front, the three of them in the rear—which definitely sounded sexier than it was. We squinted into the bright sunlight as we emerged from the paste factory, the truck already waiting. Said truck was massive, all white, all metal, no identifying marks. Heck, it didn't even have tires or windows. Basically, it was a large, floating, metal box.

"Our chariot awaits," said Dad glumly.

I matched his glum with a gloom as we closed the gap between us and the hovering behemoth. The side of the box parted, revealing the interior, revealing a cage within. Misery quickly trumped glum and gloom.

I turned to the others just before we boarded. I thought to say something inspiring, something along the lines of "it's always darkest before the dawn," only, it came out as, "Um…"

Not that I didn't mean to finish the thought, to, you know, inspire, but I'd been interrupted. That is to say, weapons started firing at us from all sides. Or at least three sides. And not at us so much as at the guards. Laser-like beams shot out, striking the menacing trio behind us. They fell down in a heap. *Kerplunk*! The melee lasted barely a minute, more meh than melee

"Um," I repeated.

"Yeah, um," said Craig with an added, "What the fuck?"

"Language!" shouted Mom from her concealed vantage point.

"It's English!" shouted Cher from her concealed vantage point.

I grinned, missing Tag all the more, knowing he would've said the exact same thing. "How?" I said, staring from them to the armed guards. "You…you killed them."

Britney appeared from behind her own concealed vantage point. "Not killed. Stunned. If we wanted to kill, there wouldn't be bodies left." I grimaced at the imagery. "As to how, you contacted us. We traced you back to here. We gathered the weapons we still had from the government prison. We saw the prison truck, figured you were to be loaded into it, hid, and…" She pointed toward the downed guards. "Easy." She smiled. "And you're welcome."

Craig ran up to her and hugged her. The kiss sort of threw me off. Butterflies flittered and fluttered inside my gut. I smiled at the kiss, then blushed just a bit as it lingered. I waited for either Mom or Dad to say something, but they, too, were kissing. I turned to Sonny and Cher. Yep, kisses all around. Meaning, not ones to be left out, Milo and I were kissing as well, even though neither of us had rescued the other. When in Rome, I figured—or, you know, Planet Six.

Still, we didn't have all the time in the world—or worlds, plural.

"Better get going," I said, lips unlocked.

They all nodded. They all looked at the floating metal box, its door still open. I turned to Milo. "They know about us. About me and you. Now, with what we've done here, they probably know about all of us. Hopefully, they don't know about J.T. All that said, can that—" I pointed to the truck "— help us with all this?" I then pointed to, well, everything else.

He seemed to think about it before replying. The standard

shrug quickly followed. "It's, as you call it, armored. It should offer us adequate protection. Perhaps, therefore, it can be used to our advantage." He looked inside. "Plus, it's big enough for all of us." The shrug rose north. "So yes, I say we take it." He ran back to the downed guards before ripping their ID badges off their uniforms. "Just in case," he added, then hopped on the truck. "All aboard!"

Suffice it to say, we all hopped, the door closing behind us. And just in the nick of time, too, because the wall inside was a giant monitor, and the outside was almost immediately swarming with guards, new ones, and all with weapons. Weapons, it should be noted, that were already firing at us. Thankfully, said weapons were having little effect, other than to jangle my nerves and make the box go *ping, ping, ping, ping*.

"See," said Milo, exhaling once he realized we hadn't been blown up. "Armored." He shot me a wink. I, naturally, popped a boner. Apparently, my prick didn't know we were being fired upon at the time. Either that or simply didn't care. Me, I cared.

"Anyone know how to drive this thing?" I asked.

Britney raised her hand. "The orphanage has a similar vehicle, though one that is no longer armored. It has gone from what you call a truck to what you call a bus. I watched the driver," she said. "I believe I can operate this vehicle." Her English, it seemed, had improved, though she still sounded a bit robotic. Ironically, the one almost-robot I knew, namely Tag, sounded more human than she did.

In any case, there were several more *pings* pinging all around us. "Hurry," I told her, "before our luck runs out."

Britney grabbed one of the ID badges and held it up to the screen. In an instant, the beast roared to life. That is to say, in complete silence, it began to drive off. Our young friend then ran her hands this way and that. The truck, it seemed, could detect her motions and respond in kind.

"Look at the screen, Milo," Sonny said.

Milo looked, then squinted, then smiled. "Weapons controls." He turned to me. "This baby is fully armed, Randy."

I looked, squinted, and promptly frowned. "It's also a sitting duck." All the Cureans looked my way. Clearly, they didn't understand the reference. I sighed, and amended with, "They can see us coming from a mile away."

Britney laughed. FYI, that did not sound robotic. She turned to me, her hand still twirling in the air. "Bottom right. The icon that looks like a backward letter P. Run your hand across it."

I nodded. "This vehicle usually takes two people to control it, huh?"

She nodded. "That's okay, we have eight!"

I smiled at her enthusiasm, then ran my hand across the backward letter P. Nothing happened. "Nothing happened."

"No?" she said, then spoke to the screen. "Show us the outside of the vehicle."

The monitor had been showing us the road in front of us; now we were seeing, well, nothing. Zilch, nada, zip. "I don't get it," I said.

Craig snickered. "Shock." He pointed at the screen. "There's nothing to see. You obviously ran your hand across a cloaking command, dude." He stood next to Britney, his left hand on her lower back. "They can't see us anymore, right?"

She nodded. "Right, dude."

I cringed at the word. *Oh please, dear God, not another one of them.* "What about radar, an electronic way to see us, apart from visual?"

She shrugged. "The icon you activated says cloaking. A reasonable person would surmise that that means we are cloaked, fully." She briefly looked my way and smiled. "Duh, dude."

My cringe went cringier. "Craig is a bad influence on you, Britney."

"You say potato, dude," she replied.

I turned away and sat on a bench that appeared from the floor. "I think I liked you better before you learned English."

Milo sat down next to me, his hand on my knee. Our parents were sitting in the cell. It was roomier in there, if not a bit creepier. "We need a plan, Randy," he said. "In theory, Tag will find a way to destroy the portal. If such is the case, then what? And what if Tag doesn't find a way? Or what if Tag goes...missing?"

My cringe turned wince, with a squirm thrown in for good measure. "For all intents and purposes, we're in a tank, Milo. We have weapons. They're in a building we know isn't indestructible, mainly because we destructed half of it already." I sighed as I placed my hand over his. "Let's wait to hear from J.T. or Tag. If we hear from neither, we can simply try to blow the place up." Hopefully, fingers and toes crossed, without our friends in and/or near it at the time.

He pointed around the tank. "Armored," he said. "So are they, and probably more so than ever."

Which meant that the entire human race was in the hands of Tag—Tag, who had no hands. Funny, I know. Plus, Tag was, at that very moment, flowing through a paste pipe, perhaps never to emerge again.

In short—yeah, good luck with that now—Lord help us.

Chapter 13

We drove from the factory and back to the city. It wasn't a long drive. Still, we passed several other trucks on the way, all of them heading the way we had just come from, all, more than likely, looking for us. We held our breaths every time one went by in a near-silent whizz.

"How are we moving without wheels?" I thought to ask, after the fourth truck drove by.

"The city is built on steel. The truck is magnetized," replied Cher as she sat in the cell, holding Sonny's hand. "The technology is simple enough."

I shrugged. "If you say so."

In any case, it seemed that the cloaking device was working. None of the trucks stopped and fired at us, no bombs bursting in air. *Phew.* Though we'd quickly noticed that all of the connections to the government were now lost in the vehicle. In other words, we had basic Internet, but nothing more. So, they clearly knew what we'd done, and had limited us as best they could—the fuckers.

Soon enough, we were parked outside the government building. There were guards everywhere. Britney passed her hand across the screen and gave a few commands. The building showed up on the wall, its weapons system made visible.

Britney sighed. "They have far more weapons than we do. Plus, they, like us, are heavily armored."

"Meaning," said I dolefully, "our weapons will be useless on them."

"Unless…" said Craig.

I nodded, knowing the *unless* all too well. "Unless, Tag comes up with a plan."

They all nodded in sync as we counted down the minutes until Tag's imminent rescue. Um, hopeful rescue, that is—fingers and innumerable toes crossed.

"Why are your eyes crossed?" asked Craig.

I shook my head. "Never mind."

"Stop it," said Mom. "They might stay that way."

I uncrossed them. Vanity, thy name is Randy. And then we continued to wait, and wait some more.

"It's time," eventually whispered Sonny as he stared down at his watch.

I sucked in my breath and said yet another prayer. Now that I was officially an unofficial bald and black-bedecked monk, I hoped I had a party line into the Big Guy Upstairs. Prayer quickly completed, I again gazed down at Sonny's watch. "Connect to Justin Timberlake," I croaked out.

The watch obeyed, blinking like Tag was prone to do, only with much less, you know, *personality*. More seconds ticked by, then more. My heart pounded all the while. My heart, in fact, felt like an entire percussion section. My throat was so dry it could give the Gobi a lesson or two. More seconds passed, more.

"Answer," I rasped, my face just above the device.

"Answer," said them all, one by one, as they amassed behind me. "Answer."

I tried to swallow. It hurt. I tried to blink. I couldn't.

"He's not…" I started to say, and then, praise be…

"Hello," whispered Justin Timberlake, his face appearing atop the watch. He looked like he was in some sort of closet.

"Where are you?" I asked.

"Storage closet," he replied, still in a whisper, nothing but his (hot) face in the frame. "Didn't want anyone to see or hear me. We only have a short while before my absence is noticed."

"Tag," I rasped. "Do you have Tag?"

He smiled. He lifted my friend into view. Tag blinked—with personality. "Sticky, but in one piece," said Tag.

I finally exhaled, as did the group behind me, their collective breaths hitting the back of my neck like a gust of wind. "Good to hear your voice, Tag," I said.

Again, he blinked. "And, as a side note, travelling through a pipe of paste is not the least bit enjoyable."

I grinned. "I'd think not."

Justin Timberlake came back on. "I heard what you all did, even from in here," he said. "Either insanely smart or simply insane."

"I'd say fifty/fifty."

Tag piped in with, "Fifteen/eighty-five."

My grin faltered. I liked my odds better. "In any case, how long will it take you to do what you're there to do?" Should anyone be able to hear what was being said, I was purposely being vague, even though I was dying to tell him that we were parked just outside.

Tag briefly paused. "Calculating," he said, then, "I should have the information in approximately three hours. I can access some of the databases here. I have something of a sense of the layout of this side of the building. With Justin Timberlake's help, I should be able to find the *you know what* and have our answer shortly thereafter." Seemed that Tag was also being vague. Considering how precise he normally was, how precise he was programed to be, I'm sure that *vague* was difficult for him to pull off. "I will contact you when I have an answer. After that, I will exit with Justin Timberlake, then eventually be returned to you." Again, he paused. "I miss my friends."

I gulped. He missed us. I looked over at Milo. "Still think he's just a program?"

Milo shrugged. "We miss you, too, Tag," he said into Sonny's watch. "Now, hurry back."

"I will do my best," came the reply just before said watch went blank.

I smiled. Tag's best, after all, was pretty fucking awesome. I stood and addressed the others. "Well, I guess we wait."

They all nodded, all but Britney. She, in fact, was frowning and madly waving her hands in front of the screen. "No," she said.

"What's wrong?" said Mom as she turned and stood by our young friend. "What are all those red marks on the screen."

The screen, at the time, was showing the outline of our vehicle. Red marks kept appearing and disappearing. Britney briefly looked our way. It was cool in the truck, but she was sweating. Meaning, so was I, all too soon.

"What are they, Britney?" I asked, standing by her other side.

"The government," she replied. "They're trying to find us. Each of those marks is a direct hit." She pointed at the screen. "They appear and disappear because they aren't connecting. Should they connect, the mark will remain." She turned my way. "Everything is a code, Randy. Should they break the code, we're, as you say, screwed."

"But the cloaking device," I said.

She shook her head. "This is a government vehicle. They're the government."

Sonny sighed loudly from behind me. "It's only a matter of time."

Britney's shake turned nod. "Yes, plus…"

I groaned. "Plus what?"

She pointed at Sonny's wrist. "If they capture us, they'll scan our devices. They'll know what we're up to. They'll arrest Justin Timberlake. They'll destroy Tag. They'll probably kill us all."

"Probably?" I asked, despite, one, knowing the answer, and, two, not wanting to hear the answer.

"Definitely," said Britney, followed by Cher, then Sonny, then Milo, all saying the same.

"So," I said, "What should we do? Can we get outside their

range?"

"Their range goes beyond this planet," said Sonny.

My groan returned. "So, that's a no."

"No," the Cureans all replied.

Dad tapped my shoulder. "I have an idea, but I'm not sure it's a safe one. I mean, right now, we're out of harm's way."

I turned to look at him. "Yeah, but for how much longer?"

"What is it?" asked Mom as she turned his way. "What's your idea?"

Dad sighed. "If they thought we were already dead, they'd stop looking for us."

Silence filled the space around us. We had to let Dad's words sink in. "The truck," Milo eventually said. "If it were to be destroyed, they'd think we were dead. Since they know we're all together now, they'd think we were all dead. Presumably, they'd think that all our devices were also destroyed, that even Tag was dead." He smiled at my father. "Brilliant idea, sir." His smile grew wider. "I think I can, as you'd say it, put some icing on that cake." He turned my way. "This cake thing any good, by the way."

"Depends," I replied. "Then again, compared to your paste, even a pizza with anchovies would be good." I held up my hand. "Yes, anchovies are that gross." I grinned his way. "Now, what's that icing thing?"

He looked at Britney. "If we fired our weapons, would the cloaking device be momentarily deactivated?" She nodded. "And could you fire on a timer, say if we're not in the truck at the time?" Again, she nodded.

"Brilliant," said Dad.

A faint blush spread across Milo's cheeks. "Must be contagious, sir."

"But wait," said Mom. "We can't fire at the building in front of us. Tag is in there. Justin Timberlake is in there. Plus, it's armored."

Milo nodded. "This is a government vehicle. What if we queried the truck, found out where their system controls are? The building Tag is in, Justin Timberlake is in, it's a prison, not a weapon's control center. Whatever is protecting the prison, theoretically, must be someplace else. If we found that place, then we could fire everything we have there, possibly do some damage, possibly also weaken the defenses of the prison."

I patted his shoulder. Flesh met flesh. Three-two-one contact. In other words, fine, despite the circumstances, which were dire at best, I popped a boner—with my parents and brother a foot away. Thankfully, Curean clothes were, shall we say, *protective.* "One more time: brilliant."

"Yeah, well," he said. "That Z chromosome does come in handy."

Craig snickered as he pointed my way. "Not for everybody."

I ignored the comment as I turned to Britney. She was already waving her hands, images on the screen flashing by, lightning fast. "Locked," she said. "Everything locked, protected." Her hands kept frantically waving, grabbing at the air, flicking this way and that. All the while, the images kept racing by. We all waited, breaths so baited they could catch a school of fish. Then, at last, an image remained frozen on the screen. Britney's face was red by that point, but at least she was finally smiling. "There," she said, pointing dead ahead. "I entered through an old system. Thankfully, the building we seek is, um, *old.*"

FYI, it was big and metal, gleaming in its newishness. It looked like all the other buildings I'd seen. If it was old, it hid its age well. In any case, there it was and here we were and there we would soon be.

"How far?" I asked.

Britney again waved her hands. "Two Earth hours, total, there and back."

My groan returned. "But we need to be there and then get back here," I said.

Mom also groaned. "And we won't have the truck anymore."

Dad's groan made it an unhappy trio. "And we'll be two hours away from here, away from Tag, away from Justin Timberlake. What if they need us?"

Milo raised his hand. "And how are we going to make it back here?" He pointed at the screen. "That's just outside the city. No public transportation. Plus, we're on wanted posters everywhere by now. That's a long time to be outside in the open, if we can even find a way back."

I grinned as I pointed at all the men. "Yeah, but we're not monks on any of those posters."

"Brilliant," said Milo.

Craig, of course, rolled his eyes. "First time for everything."

"But what about us women?" asked Mom.

I looked at Milo. "I seem to recall hearing about nuns on Planet Six."

He grinned. "Yes." A chuckle spewed forth, lighting my soul like a torch in the darkness. Sappy, sure, but true. "And bald as well, red clothes instead of black."

Mom gulped. "Bald?"

I patted her arm. "You'll match Dad."

"Bald?" she repeated.

"You'll match me and Craig," I tried.

She stared at me. "But bald?"

"Nuns eat fruit and vegetables."

I turned to him, nonplussed. "Wait, what?"

"Fruits and vegetables," he replied. "Those are the correct words, right? Food produced by trees, by the soil?"

I blinked. "Yes, those are the correct words. But why do we eat paste if you have fruits and vegetables."

He shrugged. "We eat what is provided; the nuns eat only of the earth. It is the old way, the way of their order."

I turned to Mom. "You should've gone bald sooner."

She nodded. "Worth it." She gulped. "Probably."

Oh, hell to the no, no probably about it; I'd take bald over paste anytime. ANYTIME!

§ § § §

So, that's how we wound up at yet another secret government building, five of us dressed in black, three of us in red, all of us very much bald, five of us smiling like cats, post-canary, three of us frowning like canaries, post-cat. And I think you can guess who was who in that scenario.

Dad rubbed Mom's head. "You look beautiful, honey."

"I look like Sinead O'Connor."

"Who?" I asked.

She frowned. "Please don't," she said, looking baldly miffed.

I shrugged. I thought she looked pretty nifty, actually. Hipster cool. Especially in all that snug red. In any case, I turned to Britney. "Ready?"

Once again, her hands were waving at the screen as if she'd seen a friend she hadn't run into in ages. In other words, or word, frantically. "Almost," she said. "Everyone vacate. I'll be outside in a minute. Then walk away fast because I can, it seems, only program this truck for five Earth minutes out."

I gulped. "That enough time to get away?"

She shrugged. "Guess we'll find out."

We all stared at her as if she was crazy. Then again, all of this was crazy, so her comment was simply par for the course.

In any case, as she'd told us to, we vacated. Bye-bye truck; hello open road.

Another minute later, she joined us. A second later, five monks and three nuns could be seen racing down said open road. Somewhere in all that, there was a joke. Sadly, no one was in a joking mood—present company included. I mean, you tell a joke when your heart is racing like Seabiscuit running a final lap and sweat is flowing down your back like the mighty Mississippi.

A minute went by.

Two minutes went by.

Three minutes went by.

If you're sensing a pattern here, bravo for you.

So, let's just skip ahead.

Five minutes went by.

And then…*BOOOOOM!*

The truck, as planned, had shot out every weapon in its arsenal. I know this because, though said arsenal was largely silent, the explosions that soon occurred were not. Was the building we fired at armored? I suppose it was, though it clearly was no match for our truck. Maybe because the building was old and had never been upgraded. Or maybe the government never figured that anyone would try to blow it up. Either way, blow up it did. Like I said, *BOOOOOM!*

One minute we were racing and sweating, the next, we were being flung out and down, fire and smoke and debris whooshing up into the sky in an inferno we only thankfully tangentially felt and smelled and heard. So yes, a five-minute head start was enough, if only by a hair. The only casualty was our truck, which had been blown up by the enemy just as the enemy was also being blown up, as planned.

We all slowly rose and quickly turned.

Eyes wide, we then all stared at each other, smiles slowly rising up our sweaty, dusty, monky, nunny, faces.

"Huh," I said.

Craig nodded. "Yep, huh."

The building was toast. The building, in fact, was a whole factory of Wonder Bread toast.

We all cheered our success. And since we were finally in a joking mood, here you go:

A monk and a nun are throwing darts inside a monastery. The monk throws his dart and misses the board. "Oh shit, I missed," the monk says.

To which the nun says, "Don't say that here; this is a holy place."

The monk assures her that he will not say it again and throws his next dart. It misses the board. "Oh shit, I missed."

The nun then exclaims, "Do not say that here. The Lord will smite you." And, as if to back up the claim, thunder rumbles in the distance.

"Okay, okay," says the monk, "I won't say it again."

The monk throws the third dart and again misses the board. "Oh shit, I missed."

All at once, lightning strikes the nun. A rumbling voice from heaven then booms out, "Oh shit, I missed."

§§§§

The joking mood quickly faded. We were, after all, outside the city, bald, dusty, and very much without transportation. FYI, Planet Six didn't have cabs or Uber. Also FYI, hitchhiking probably wouldn't work, what with there being eight of us, and all. And so, we began to walk, and fast, because the government would soon be looking for the perpetrators, namely us.

We moved off the road, finding a path through a stretch of orange grass. There was barely any traffic, but it was safer to not be spotted. I mean, five monks and three nuns along the side of the road was a pretty conspicuous sight—or so I'm guessing.

Twenty minutes later, we saw a farm. I mean, I was guessing it was a farm. It looked, you know, farmy. Sterile-looking, sure, but farmy just the same.

"Farm," said Milo.

See!

"How do you know?" asked my mom. "I don't see any crops or animals?"

Milo pointed down. "Crops."

Craig scratched his head. "This orange stuff?"

Milo nodded. "They make the paste out of it."

I shook my head. I breathed in. It smelled fresh there, rather nice, actually. And the grass was the most beautiful shade of orange. Carrotty, in fact. "This, this pretty grass makes that awful grey paste?"

Cher nodded as she reached down and ran her hands through it, smiling all the while. "Among other things, or so I've heard."

Weird, I thought. Such a nice grass, such gross paste. I reached down and yanked at it, a handful soon in my palm. I took a munch. I promptly spit it out, my face scrunched up as I spat and spat and spat some more.

"Nope," I said with a grimace. "Tastes just like the paste, only orangier." Figured, right?

Still, all was not hopeless. We soon approached a house. It was metal, large. Best of all, there was a floating metal box off to its side. Was it a truck, a bus, a tractor? No clue. It was a box. It was floating. There was so little variety on Planet Six, even in their vehicles. It was a beautiful world. It was a boring world. Everyone was stunning. It all seemed so wasted.

I loved Milo. I wished I could save him from this place, but, if things turned out as planned, I'd be as trapped here as he was, as they all were.

Still, for the time being, we had bigger fish to fry. Or, you know, floating boxes to pilfer. Was I loathe to steal? Let me ask you a better question: was I loathe to blow up a government building? Better still: was I eager to save my entire planet? Yeah, so there's your answer: greater good, people. Greater good. Plus, if I'd thought about it too much, I would've probably gone crazy. In other words, I was acting, not thinking. Worked for me.

Which is why we were sneaking into the floating box a moment later. Turned out, it wasn't a truck or a bus or a tank. Nope, it was— be still my heart—a food transport vehicle. And that sucker was stock full of fruits and vegetables of every size and shape and smell and texture. And yes, my Curean friends had to inform me of this because none of it looked like any sort of fruit or vegetable I'd ever seen before.

I went to eat one, when Cher's hand landed on mine. "Illegal," she said.

I grinned. "We're steeling the vehicle we're in, Cher. We just blew up a government building." She removed her hand. I held a round, purple fruit to my mouth—though, hey, it could've been a vegetable. "So yeah, I'm going to illegally be eating this. I mean, this purple beauty isn't weighing too heavily on my soul right about now."

I chomped down. I moaned involuntarily. I hadn't eaten anything but paste for far too long. This fruit—or was it a vegetable?—was pure, unadulterated heaven, its juices flowing down my chin as I took another massive bite. I suddenly wished there were words that rhymed with purple so that I could write a poem about it.

"Oh my God," I finally uttered. "What the hell is this?"

Milo looked at the fruit or vegetable hungrily. He told me the word for it. There were far too many consonants for something that tasted so yummy. I held it up to him. Oddly, he backed away. "Like my mother said, it's illegal. Food is only for the nuns."

I grinned. I handed something bright and shiny and pink to Cher. "Well then, thankfully, we have a few on board."

Britney was pulling the vehicle away from the farm as Cher reluctantly took the proffered food. She smiled at me shyly. "First time," she said.

"For this particular…"

"Fruit," she said.

"Yes, first time for this fruit?"

Milo shook his head. "We have never eaten anything but paste. Ever. None of us. No one but the nuns."

My eyes went wide. I took a bite of something half blue, half green. It was even more extraordinary than the purple thing. I held the remainder to him. He held it to his mouth. Cher had a pink edible held to hers. Mother and son at last bit into the forbidden fruit. Or maybe it was the forbidden vegetable. Either way, they bit, eyes fluttering as soon as the juices hit their tongues.

"*Mmm,*" said Cher, a smile spreading wide across her exquisite face.

"God," said Milo, mouth full as he chewed.

I nodded and took a bite of something yellow with swirls of red. "Yeah, this'll make you believe in a higher power, for sure."

Britney turned from the driver's seat. Not that there was an actual seat, but still. "Toss me something!"

I tossed. She ate. I tossed. Sonny ate. I tossed and tossed. Mom and Dad ate. In other words, in seconds, we were devouring the fruit and/or vegetables. And then—surprise, surprise—I had my own brilliant idea, which, for now, I was keeping to myself. Mainly because I like to spring my brilliance on people. That's because, like the Spring, I only bloom for such a short period each year.

In any case, we were once again on track, heading to the city, heading to Tag, to Justin Timberlake, to the, *gulp,* unknown.

To our fates, really.

Heck, even to your fate, right?

§ § § §

Halfway back, Sonny's watch beeped.

In all the excitement, and with our chins various shades of yellow and green and red and blue and orange, we almost forgot about Tag's mission. At once, everyone stopped eating and stared at Sonny's watch.

"Hello?" Sonny said into it.

"Sonny," Tag said. "Hello to you as well. I have news."

It was nice to hear his voice. Terrifying, but nice. "Of the good variety or the bad?" I asked.

"Not possible to say yet," he replied. "For now, simply news."

"Spill it," said Craig.

"Spill?" said Tag. "I have nothing to spill. In fact, I can't hold anything in order to be able to spill. It is one of my few flaws. I cannot sing all that well either. Monotone does not translate well to harmony."

I held up my hand for him to stop, even though he couldn't see it. "Just tell us the news, please."

"Right," he said. "I found the portal." We all clapped. We all cheered. We all promptly stopped clapping and cheering when he said, "There is a self-contained system protecting it. It is impossible to break into it from the outside. It is also heavily armored. I have never seen the technology. It does not exist in any databases. I am not sure what weapon can destroy it. Such a weapon, if it exists, I can only assume, would also destroy much of the surrounding city, thereby killing innocent civilians."

"We have no weapons anymore, anyway, Tag," I told him. "Besides what we stole from the prison, we have nothing. And I doubt those can help us now." I sighed. "Can't Justin Timberlake help us? Maybe somehow turn off the protective system?"

Justin Timberlake answered for himself. "I am a scientist, Randy. I have no knowledge of such systems. I have no access to anything beyond my lab. I was able to walk Tag around, allow his systems to access what he could, but beyond that, we have exhausted all other possibilities."

I nodded. We had one other option then. "The invasion will occur there, though," I said. "It has to. And when it does, the protective system will be deactivated. Only then will we be able to destroy the portal."

"That is correct," said Tag. "Though one would assume that, at that time, every spare weapon in this building will be aimed at anyone trying to approach. And to use your wording—or perhaps *lettering*—FYI, they have amassed a formidable arsenal here; that much I have seen."

We all sighed as one. I changed the subject. "When will the invasion occur?"

"Not sure of the time," said Tag. "But based on the movement within the building, with the level of urgency, with the number of government employees now in the building, I would say shortly."

I nodded. "On a hopeful bright note, we were, I think, able to destroy their central operating system. Can you tell if the building's security, outside of the portal's, is still operational?"

"Let me check, Randy," he replied. There was silence on his end for a half a minute or so. "Deactivated," he said. "Apart from the weapons inside, this building is now unguarded." He chuckled. I loved hearing him do so. "How did you manage this?"

My chuckle joined his. "Long story, Tag. And I'm afraid time is running out as it is." My chuckle turned to a laugh. "Plus, we ate fruit. I think. Though it might've been vegetables." I paused. I whispered into Sonny's wrist. "I think it, the food, might be our only hope."

To which he whispered back, "Are most humans this crazy, Randy?"

I nodded. "Probably, Tag. But I'm not most humans; I'm the savior."

Yep, Craig's eyes went arollin'. "Full of yourself much?"

"He is the savior," said Justin Timberlake. "Perhaps he was simply meant to save your world instead of ours."

Craig, it seemed, was going to say something snarky in reply, then reconsidered. I think it was because Mom lightly slapped his arm before he could. Or maybe it was because Dad lightly slapped his other arm. Either way, snarky flew out the proverbial window. Which was odd because Planet Six didn't seem to have any windows.

"You guys need to get out of there," I said. "If the invasion is happening soon, and the portal needs to be destroyed, you need to be with us."

"Agreed," said Justin Timberlake. "But the building is now on lockdown."

A groan went up within the truck. "Look for the diversion, sir," I told him. "Look for it and then find us." I grinned. "We're easy to spot now, by the way: five monks and three nuns."

"Excuse me?" said J.T.

"Yes, what he said," said Tag.

My grin widened as I took my friends and family in. "Part of that long story I mentioned. In any case, when the time comes, run; run and find us."

"We will," said Tag. "But hurry, Randy. Please, hurry."

The watch went blank. My heart went *boom*. Hurry, he said. Sadly, there were quite a few limiting factors in that regard.

Chapter 14

We temporarily left the truck and found ourselves in yet another skyrise. I turned to Britney once we were all safely in an apartment. "Last project for you," I told her.

"Sounds a bit too final for my liking, dude," she said. "How about: current project."

I nodded. "Either way, can you break into the system in here and communicate with the entire city?"

Everyone in the room turned to me. "Huh?" Craig said. "Why do we need to do that?"

I hadn't told them by plan, not yet. Not until I knew we could pull it off first. If Britney couldn't do what I was asking, we'd have to come up with a new plan. Seeing as my brilliance was short-lived, said new plan had yet to be formulated. In other words, all my eggs were in that shoddy basket of ours.

"Humor me," I said to them all.

Britney squinted my way, clearly thinking of how to pull such an idea off. "Only the government is able to communicate with the entire city at once, in case of an emergency."

"Such as?" asked Mom.

"War," Britney said.

"And when was the last time your people were in a war?" asked Dad.

To which Sonny replied, "Nearly sixteen-hundred years ago."

I sighed. "Any other time they need to mass-communicate."

She nodded. "Weather. Planet Six occasionally has massive dust storms. If the power goes out, which is next to near impossible, the inhabitants go without food. If a dust storm is predicted that has the potential to wipe out the power grid, the city is notified to amass enough paste to last a week."

"And where does this warning generate from then?" I asked.

Britney looked to Cher. Cher looked to Sonny. Sonny looked to Milo. Milo looked to Britney. In other words, where was Tag when you needed him.

"Your watch, Sonny," I said. "Is it like Milo's?"

Sonny smiled. "Strangely, no watch is quite like Milo's. I believe there was a malfunction during his assemblage."

I grinned. That explained a lot. "Still, is it relatively like Milo's? Because we can't communicate with Tag right now. Too dangerous."

Sonny shrugged. "More or less the same," he said, holding up his wrist. "Materialize," he then said.

Sonny's watch pulsed with light before shooting out a Hologram that looked like Jennifer Lawrence, only with bigger boobs. "You picked out the design, right?" I said.

Sonny's face reddened. "To be fair, my wife allowed it."

Cher smirked. "To be fair, I chose the home model. The home model is a male. The home model, therefore, has significantly smaller breasts."

"And hates me," said Sonny.

Cher shrugged. "Must also be a malfunction." She winked my way.

I smiled and turned to the hologram. "Please determine where weather alerts generate from. Please bring up that system on the wall. Please do not connect to the buildings operating system while doing so."

Milo nodded. "Smart," he said. "Don't potentially alert the government to our doings." He stopped nodding. "What, exactly, are your doings?"

I held my index finger up to my lips. "Wait," I told him. "Let's see if Britney can do this first."

"Do what, though?" she asked.

I looked her way. "You need to break into the weather alert system. You need to break in and we need to take control of it. Only the city's population needs to be contacted. Is that all possible?"

She grinned, her hands already at the ready. "What do you think, dude?"

I knew what I thought. I thought: *you're so fucked, weather alert system.* And then I again turned to the hologram, who appeared frozen, boobs at a standstill as she apparently searched for a solution to my query.

Two minutes later, the wall lit up like a Fourth of July parade. The hologram smiled mechanically and mechanically replied, "The weather alert system is now active, sir." She pointed at the wall, her hand glowing, see-through. "Is this what you desired, sir?" She sounded oddly sexy, all of a sudden. I had a strong feeling that Sonny's programming was involved. I had a strong feeling because Sonny was smiling and Cher was not.

"Off," said Cher, then turned my way as the hologram promptly twinkled and vanished. "I like Tag a lot better."

I nodded. "Makes two of us." I turned to Britney. "Go for it."

Her hands began to move, up, down, left, right, in circles. "Give me an hour. I need to get in and not let them know I'm in. That takes a little more time."

I looked at Milo as he looked at me. My smile matched his.

"See you in an hour," I said to the group. "We need to, uh, work on the plan."

Yep, brotherly eyes rolled. "Give me a break."

Milo looked at me with a shrug. "Still sounds painful."

I grabbed Milo's hand and rushed us out of there. Linguistics was so not to be on the menu.

§§§§

We were in the apartment next door a minute later. We were naked in even less time that.

"Before you fuck me, Randy," he said, "I think we should talk."

I sighed. My boner did the same. "Can't we talk after I fuck you. Or during? Or perhaps both?"

He shook his head. He pulled me in and down, a bed appearing beneath us before we hit the floor. No, I didn't exactly love Planet Six, but the technology was easy enough to get used to. And yes, I did exactly love Milo, so the bed was doubly appreciated.

He rolled on top of me and pressed his lips down on mine. The world around us instantly faded and vanished. God might have belched four universes into existence, but in that kiss, we had created a fifth. Sorry about it, God.

"I love you, Randy," he said, once said kiss was broken.

"I love you, too, Milo," I replied. "And?"

"*And* if this plan of yours works, you'll be trapped here. Your whole family will be trapped here."

"I know; we discussed that already."

He nodded. He sighed. He kissed me. There was that fifth universe again. "Yes, but, if you're trapped here, and if the portal is forever closed, my government isn't going to stop until we're all dead."

My eyes went wide. This we had not discussed. This, in fact, hadn't crossed my mind. "Oh," I managed to squeak out.

"Yeah, oh," he replied.

I had to stop for a moment. I had to think about what he said. Trapped was one thing. Not seeing our world was one thing, too. But being on the run until we all died was a far greater thing. Plus, this didn't involve just me and Milo; there were eight of us in this mess, eight lives irrevocably tied together. Ten, if you included Tag and Justin Timberlake. We'd all be on the run. All of us. Forever. Forever eating, *blech*, paste.

I blinked. I looked into his limpid pools of blue. I smiled. I knew the answer. I had it, in fact, as soon as he said he loved me and I said I loved him. "Fate brought us together, Milo," I said, "but I'll be damned if some paste-pushing government will ever tear us apart. Besides, I'm the savior. Maybe that means I'm here to save all of us."

He smiled and ground his ass into my crotch. "You already saved me, just by being here."

"Same here," I replied, maneuvering my body, his body, my cock, his hole. It all took ten seconds, by the way. FYI, that was ten seconds too long for me. "Talk over now?"

He shrugged as my cock slid inside, said shrug joined by a rapturous moan. "Talk over," he groaned.

"Thank God," I said.

And I did.

And I did again, just in case he didn't hear me the first time.

§ § § §

An hour later, we were all back together again. I was equal parts relaxed and tense. Still, better than being a hundred percent tense, right? I mean, if the end of the word was nigh—and I was seriously hoping for no on the whole nigh thing—then at least I would go with something of a smile on my face.

"Well?" I asked, staring at Britney, her hands at last at rest.

She shrugged. "T'weren't nothin'."

I grinned. "When did you have time to learn slangy American Western?"

She pointed at Craig. "He taught me cowboys and Indians."

I cringed. I prayed she wasn't speaking sexually. Judging from my parent's expressions, I wasn't the only one praying at the time—and God was busy enough with our long list of prayers as it was. "In any case, you're in?"

She nodded and pointed at the wall. "We have access to the weather alert system. The government does not know that we have access to the weather alert system." She grinned and bowed my way. "Giddy up, little doggie."

I smiled and gazed up at the wall. "Wall," I said. "Keyboard, please." Thankfully, the wall knew what I was asking for. Sadly, the keyboard was in Cureal. "In English, please." The wall glimmered for a moment. The keyboard turned to English. I typed on the wall. When I was done, I amassed the seven of them, bald ladies in the front, bald men in the back, red in the first row, black in the second. I pointed at the wall, at what I had written. "Cher, once I turn on the system, please read that."

They were all already reading. Thankfully, they were also all smiling after they finished.

"Diversion," said Milo.

"And a huge one," said Britney.

"Just what was called for," I said proudly.

Craig held up his hand. "Please don't say brilliant anyone; his head is already a few sizes too big, as of late."

"Still," I said, pointing at the wall. "You know…"

Craig sighed. "Fine, fine. Can we just please get this ball rolling. Invasion imminent, remember?"

I nodded. I ran to the second row, joining my fellow monks as we all stared at the wall. "Go for it, Brit."

"Weather alert system," she said, "activate and televise."

The wall again morphed. We were now staring at it as the group of us were staring back at, um, *us*. That is to say, we were being, as Britney had said, televised, seeing what the population of City Northeast Nineteen was seeing.

At last, I was a star!

Sadly, I looked like Howie Mandel at the time. In other words: bald, bald, bald. It was a startling image, to be sure. Judging by all our expressions, no one was happy with their new hairdos—or lack thereof. Still, we persevered. Or at least Cher did.

Suddenly, she was smiling, very friendly-nun-like. "Fellow Cureans," she said, reading the script on the wall, translating my words to, of course, Cureal. In English, she was saying: "For far too long, only we nuns have been offered the privilege of food, while the rest of the planet eats paste. As a sign of solidarity, our holy order has decided to share our supply with you, with the blessing of the government. Please amass at the downtown building that was recently half blown-up. Fruits and vegetables for everyone!"

Britney waved her hand. The wall again turned white. She looked at me and said, "But there's only enough food for a few dozen people at most."

I smiled and nodded knowingly. "Exactly, Brit. Exactly."

§ § § §

We left the apartment fast, before the people of the city could act on our broadcast. Fortunately, we only had to run across the street to our floating metal box, which we promptly opened and then emptied, dumping the fruits and vegetables onto the ground. It should be noted that the city was spotless. In other words, dumping the food onto the ground wasn't as gross as it sounded. Plus, beggars couldn't be choosers.

And the beggars started showing up mere moments later.

And by beggars, I mean hordes of them. Planet Six might've been dying, and the city might've been mostly empty, but when you promised everyone free food that wasn't paste, they came running, like I said, in hordes. Droves, even. Throngs might be better. Hundreds of them came pouring in from all sides, easily half the city. And though the pile of food was large, no, it'd never feed all of them. Or most of them. Or even the first batch of them.

In other words, hordes, droves, and throngs quickly became rioting droves, rampaging droves, and raging throngs.

"Where's the rest of it?!" they all shouted. Or at least I think that's what they were shouting, give or take.

We, the nuns and the monks, pointed at the building in front of us. "The government has the rest!" shouted Milo in Cureal.

The mobs paused and stared at the building. Suffice it to say, it was a very brief pause. In other words, seconds later, we, at last, had our needed diversion.

The building parted. The guards rushed out to see what the commotion was. They weren't prepared for the entirety of the city to be there. Which is to say, they weren't prepared for the influx, the flood of them, all of them shouting at full voice, hungry, it seemed, for anything other than paste.

The noise was very nearly deafening, like a tsunami rushing over you. I covered my ears. My eyes, of course, stayed glued to the unfolding scene. People kept swarming into the building, the guards falling by the wayside. After all, how do you fight a tsunami? Plus, the building was no longer armored, thanks to us, so fighting in general was now a no-go.

Still, it wasn't the ingoing flood I was concerned about; it was the outgoing.

The eight of us stood there, Cureans shouting on all sides, our food supply already long eaten, the mob now rabid for it.

"Come on," I said, clenching my fists as I stared at the entrance, watching, waiting. "Come on. Come on."

Milo was standing by my side. "Come on," he said. "Come on."

We were crushed together, all of us facing the entrance to the building, all of us doing that watching/waiting game—and less than patiently, I might add.

And then, at last, "Justin Timberlake!" I shouted, frantically waving my arms. "Justin Timberlake! Justin Timberlake! Justin Timberlake!" I felt like a groupie as I shouted his name over and over and over again.

At last, he locked eyes with me as he tried his darnedest to push through the crowd. And yes, he looked hot doing it. In fact, he looked hot for a full ten minutes, at least, which is how long it took him before he, at last, reached us, hotly huffing and puffing until he was shouting in my ear, "Is this the diversion you promised?!"

I nodded. "Yes! You like?!"

He nodded. "As diversions go, this one is rather spectacular!"

I stared into his stunning peepers before my own eyes moved to his wrist, to the watch wrapped around it. "Tag!" I shouted.

The watch lit up. "Here, Randy!" He shimmered into being, instantly standing by J.T.'s side. "The portal is still shielded, but the invading army is temporarily occupied with…" He pointed to the still swarming masses. "That will buy us some time!"

I thought to hug him. I desperately wanted to hug him, but, well, you know. Instead, I smiled and said, "I know, Tag! And glad to see you!"

He smiled in return. "You don't have to shout, Randy. I don't have ears; I have advanced technology auditory sensors. I can hear, as you might say, a cricket in a dust storm."

I laughed. "I would never say that, but got it." I tilted my head to the building. "But back to the portal. How do we destroy it?" I pointed at the mob. "Without harming any innocent bystanders."

He nodded. "Like I said, the portal has its own internal protective system. Britney can't break into it, nor can we destroy it with our weapons."

"Please tell me that's all followed with a *but*," I pled.

He smiled. It was impossible not to find his smile wondrous. "*But*," he said, "the protective system is controlled by someone, presumably the commander of this building. He must be able to activate and deactivate said system. If we can find this man, convince him to destroy the portal, then your world will at last be safe."

"Except, how do we do that?" I asked.

Tag's smile would've given the Mona Lisa pause. "I already saw this man while I was inside with Justin Timberlake."

My stomach suddenly lurched. "Please tell me that's followed with an *and*," I said.

He nodded. "*And…*" An image flickered to the side of his face.

"This is the man."

My nod mirrored his. The crowd was even more dense now, the shouting intense. Our group was pressed in tight, forming a protective ring around Tag. "I did the *but*, the *and*, now how about the *so*? *So*?"

"Yeah, so?" echoed Craig, who was standing by my side, holding Britney's hand. He looked nervous. We all did. Our fates, after all, were tied to a holographic program, albeit one who was stunningly handsome.

He lifted his index finger. He pointed at the sky. "Watch, my friends," he said, which was kind of ironic, given that he was indeed a watch.

All our faces aimed toward the heavens, the moons already visible, even in the light of day. In an instant, the face that had been pulsing by Tag's side was now projected above all our heads, everyone's, large as a movie screen.

I gulped. I didn't know what Tag had up his sleeve—and, given that he didn't even have a sleeve, I should've perhaps been weary—and yet, I still eagerly awaited something dastardly and/or genius. I was hoping for the *and*.

FYI, I wasn't disappointed.

There was a brief crackling sound before we—and by we, I mean everyone in a five-hundred-foot radius, or thereabouts—heard in Cureal, which was translated a few minute later for us humans: "People of City Northeast Nineteen, the man you see above your heads is the commander of this building. He is the one who offered you food, but clearly did not provide enough. Find him inside. Bring him here, to the people."

Oh, the sound of them then. The crowd roared. The crowd rushed. We were tossed about as if in a tempest.

"Now what, though?!" I shouted Tag's way. "He won't have food. And even if he does, how will that get the portal closed?!"

"There is food; I've seen it," came his reply. "They're readying for an invasion. They don't trust human nourishment."

I grinned knowingly. "Says the people who eat paste."

Tag shrugged. "In any case, we have a bargaining chip. Now all you need do is bargain. Plus, he already speaks English, also in preparation for the invasion."

My grin faltered. "Wait, you want me to do the bargaining? Me?" I pointed my way, just in case I wasn't being clear enough.

Dad put his hand on my shoulder and spoke into my ear, "Tag's a machine, Randy. They don't see him like you do. This commander won't bargain with him."

Mom leaned in to my other ear. "We're right behind you, Randy. Don't worry; everything will be alright."

I turned to look at her. "You really think so?"

She nodded. She smiled. "We're here. We're safe. We travelled between universes." Her smile grew even brighter as her hands rested on my shoulders. "Apart from the whole bald thing, fate does seem to be on our side." She rubbed her hand over her shiny dome. "Though fate seems to have a nasty sense of humor."

My nod mirrored hers. "Tell me about it."

Milo tapped me on the arm. I turned and gazed into his eyes. It was the same every time, butterflies swarming inside my belly as the connection was made. He smiled. I smiled in return. "Let's do this, Randy. You're the savior; time to do some serious saving."

My brain buzzed. I started to reply, but my voice was utterly and completely drowned out by the crowd, which was pushing and shoving a man our way. Seconds later, said man was standing before us.

"Commander," I said with a nod of my head.

"You," he said, eyes wide, shocked it seemed to see me. "But how? You're, you're dead." He stared at each of us in turn. "All of you are dead. That's what was reported."

The mob hushed a bit. They didn't speak English, I supposed, but this had to be the first time in their collective lives that someone was standing up to the government—and they had ring-side seats for the show. They backed up a bit, gave us some room.

"Pretty lengthy story, that 'how' you mentioned," I replied. "Does it matter, anyway? I mean, you're here, I'm here, clearly not dead, and this crowd is ready to tear you limb from limb. That's the long and the short of it, right?" I cracked my knuckles for effect. The commander grimaced at the sound. In other words, I got my effect. Cowering would've been better, but grimacing was fine. "Now then, we need you to turn the portal security off."

He grinned menacingly. "Need? What do you know of need? My people are dying. That is need." His grimace turned to a sneer. He looked like Joseph Gordon-Levitt, only buffer, sneerier. "The portal will remain protected until it's time."

"To invade," said Dad, a matching sneer on his face. "My people won't take it too kindly, you know."

The commander shrugged. "You'll never be able to fight us. You'll die trying."

Milo pointed at me. "You have a mere four humans here…" He pointed at the nearly decimated building behind us. "Look what four can do." He pointed at the crowd surrounding us. "They're smarter than you think."

Craig promptly piped up next, adding, "Turn off the portal, or you'll be next."

The commander poked my brother in the chest. "Little boy, go bark at someone who is afraid of you."

I pushed him away. He looked surprised that someone would dare touch him. "Leave my brother alone, asshole." I pushed him again. His surprised look turned to stunned. Me, I was just as surprised, my heart pumping like crazy, but no way was this alien gonna talk shit to my little bro. "Now then, turn off the portal security, or else!"

I pushed him a third and final time. He tripped. He fell. The mob sucked in their collective breaths. If I looked surprised, and the commander looked stunned, they looked shocked. And then, several of them clapped, then more of them, then more after that, until there was a massive round of applause. For me. Wait. I mean,

FOR ME! Yes, better.

I stared at the downed commander. "Or else that. Better still, or else *them*." I pointed at the cheering masses, then moved in closer to him, staring down, our eyes locked. "Turn off the portal or we let them loose on you."

He no longer looked smug. The sneer vanished; it was replaced by a look a fear. "It is illegal to attack a government employee. They would never. They don't even know what you're fighting for. They don't even speak your language."

I turned to Tag. "Show him."

Tag glimmered. Tag smiled. Tag spoke, his voice projected all around. To translate: "This man has food. Lots of food. We, these monks and nuns, want something from him. If he does what we ask, we'll get you your food." And here he applied more of that aforementioned icing, and none of that paste shit. "It is God's will."

And since we were, theoretically, monks and nuns—monks and nuns who did God's will for a living—the mob turned from us to the man on the ground, the man now cowering in rightful fear.

"No!" he shouted in Cureal. "It is illegal. You will be punished!" Or so it was later translated to me. Either way, I got the gist. The crowd, however, didn't seem to care much for his threats. They had paste. He had real food. We were God's envoys. Enough said.

We moved back as they closed in. In an instant, he was swallowed up, the sea of them dragging him under. All we could hear were his screams and shouts, and then not even that.

I looked at Tag. "Make them stop."

He nodded. He spoke again. "Stop. That's enough." His voice boomed, seemingly from all directions. The mob, however, did not stop. "STOP!" shouted Tag, and yes, it was odd to hear him shouting. Tag, you see, was fairly even-keeled. Still, the masses continued to, uh, *mass*. Tag looked at us and said, "Cover your eyes, now." We nodded. We covered our eyes. "STOP!" he shouted, yet again, just as a blinding flash of light flared over the crowd's heads. I know it was blinding because, once we removed our hands from our faces, everyone was one the ground rubbing their clearly blinded eyes.

"Neat," said Craig as we rushed to the downed commander, who was now very much bloody and bruised and moaning up a storm.

Tag shrugged. "Easy stunt. Same one I used in the transit station bathroom. It's an emergency beacon. Tricked out, I believe you'd call it." He grinned. "This was an emergency, I suppose."

We helped the commander up. He stood on wobbly legs. "Round two?" I asked.

He waved his hands in front of his face as he vigorously shook his head. "Don't. Don't. I'll shut down the security controls. Just call them off."

Milo nodded. We all nodded. "And you'll feed them all your food," Milo said. "All of it. Seeing as you won't need it anymore."

The commander's sneer returned. "You're dooming your own people."

Milo shrugged. "I'm saving another people. Who's to say which people deserve saving more? Besides, we're not dead yet; where there's hope, there's salvation." He pointed to the sky. "And maybe God can do more than just belch this time." He then pointed to the front of the building. "Now go. Quickly. Before the mob gains their sight back and finds that you're not dead."

I could see the gulp glide down the commander's rather fetching throat. In other words, he went, and, like he was told, quickly. We, of course, followed, also quickly.

Minutes later, we entered a vast room. There were several guards, all looking at us nervously. Tag whispered in my ear, "You must have deactivated the building's weaponry in here as well. They are all that stand in the way of us and the portal."

I turned and whispered in reply, "Apart from the portal's internal security system."

He nodded. "Which will soon be deactivated."

I turned to the commander. "My people," I said. "They never would've gone down without a fight. Even if you subjugated us, we would forever rebel against you. That's what humans do. I think your people have forgotten that ability or lost it along with that nifty Y chromosome."

The commander sighed. He stared at Sonny and Cher, then at Britney and Milo, lastly at Justin Timberlake. "You'll regret this, fellow Cureans."

They smiled. "Doubtful," said Cher.

Justin Timberlake also smiled—hotly, of course. "Yes, no regrets here."

Britney shrugged. "I'm feeling pretty good about it, actually." She looked at Milo. "You?"

Milo nodded. "The government has screwed this planet up; Earth seems to still have a chance. I vote for Earth." He turned from the commander and looked at me instead. He grabbed my hand. "And for love."

Craig's eyes rolled and rolled. "Please shoot me." The commander aimed his weapon Craig's way. "Figure of speech! Figure of speech!" Craig ducked and covered.

"Butch much?" I said.

"Look who's talking, dude," replied my cowering brother.

He had a point. I let it go. We had more important matters to contend with. "Do it," I commanded the commander. "Turn it off. Now. Or else." I pointed at the wall behind us, toward the waiting mob outside.

He sighed. He walked to the wall. A control panel slid out toward him. It took a few moments of hand waving, and then said wall shimmered and promptly faded away, revealing the portal behind it.

I laughed. I couldn't help myself. "Figures," I said, gazing at said portal.

Craig laughed as well. "It looks just like ours, only bigger."

Yep, they too had created a waterfall, but one big enough to allow an invading army through it. You could see a field just beyond, through the cascading water. If I wasn't mistaken, it looked like the inside of AT&T Park, home of the Giants. That also figured, what with said park also being built of steel, just like our house.

Dad patted Craig's shoulder. Mom did the same. "Smart kid." She chuckled. "A waterfall. And inside our house, no less."

I smiled knowingly. Smart indeed. I then turned to the commander. "Now, go feed that crowd. Give them everything you have."

The commander froze. "It'll start a revolution. Only the nuns eat. If the people eat, they won't want the paste anymore."

Cher smiled. She smiled like, well, *Cher*: brilliantly, famously, *Cherly*. "Thank God," she said.

I stared at the ceiling. "Yeah, thanks, God."

Milo tapped me on the shoulder. He pointed at the portal. "You and your family can still return. We can destroy it from this side."

The smile that had been on my face suddenly vanished. "Or you and your family can come with us. Someone else can destroy the portal." I gripped his hand tightly in my own. "You'll love San Francisco. There's a restaurant on every corner. Plus, we have sealions."

"Who will destroy it?" he said. "Who would we leave behind?"

I looked at them all, my family, my extended family. I couldn't leave any of them, wouldn't.

"Me," said Tag. "Leave me. I can destroy the portal. I have access to it now that you destroyed the central operating system and the commander has lowered the shield."

I sucked in my breath. Leave Tag? But he was my friend. I tried to think rationally about it, knowing that he really was just a machine, a sophisticated program, but rationality had never been my strong point. I looked at my Mom, my Dad. "What do we do?"

They started to speak, though they never got the words out.

I mean, you try talking when the world has all of a sudden gone haywire.

Chapter 15

One minute we were all standing there, staring through the water at the ballpark's pitcher's mound, the next we were on the floor, bouncing and thrashing like fish on a pier just after they've been plucked from the sea.

"Earthquake," I said through chattering teeth. "I thought...you didn't get those...because...the city...is built...on steel."

Out of all of us, only Tag remained standing. Then again, out of all of us, Tag didn't have legs. Or feet. Or anything, really.

"No," he said. "We generally don't experience earthquakes because of the steel. Still, if the tremor is large enough, we can still feel it."

He was a blur in front of me, mainly because my head was shaking so badly. "But this is...a huge...earthquake."

He nodded. I think. "The largest." He paused. "The building's system is reporting that the universes have separated. By the feel of this quake, I'd say forever." He smiled. I think. "You saved them, Randy. Your people, our army. Had the invasion occurred, as planned, the Cureans would've been trapped, stuck for all eternity between the two universes."

I turned and stared at the commander, who was bouncing along with all of us. "You're welcome."

Milo laughed. It sounded like a series of hiccups. "You really are the savior, Randy."

I would've said that Craig's eyes were rolling, but, by that point, every part of Craig was doing just that. Still, he said, or at least managed to say, "As if…his head…isn't swollen…enough."

I smiled. I saved them. Then I frowned. "We're trapped, though." I turned and tried to focus my eyes on my parents, who were holding hands as they rattled along the floor. "We'll never see our home again."

"We're together, Randy," my Mom said. "Home is…where the heart…is."

I laughed, despite the bouncy circumstances. "Too much… Hallmark Channel…Mom."

And then, just as quickly as it had all started, the ground beneath us stopped its shaking. I looked around, waiting for aftershocks, but there were none. The commander frowned and turned to the guards, speaking in Cureal. "Gather the others. Get the food. Feed the crowd outside." The guards started to object, when the commander added, "Go. If you don't, they'll tear us apart." FYI, Milo made it sound more dramatic when he later translated all this to me—as if this shit wasn't dramatic enough already, right?

The guards hopped up and obeyed. We all hopped up and stared at the portal. The water was still waterfalling, but there was nothing beyond, no pitcher's mound, no anything. In other words, no Earth.

I looked at the commander. "Again, you're welcome."

The commander smiled. "Thank you," he said as he walked to the wall, which parted a moment later. Another moment after that, he was holding a weapon. And another moment after that, he was firing said weapon. I winced as an explosion of red shot through the air and blasted the watch off Justin Timberlake's wrist. It flung to the floor, burnt and charred. "And you're all under arrest." He kicked the watch's remains as I yelped. "And so much for the savior to the savior."

"Tag," I exhaled in a sob. I glared at the commander. "You killed our friend."

He laughed meanly. "Stupid human." He aimed the weapon my way. "He was already dead, you all were, as soon as you entered this room. You doomed yourselves the moment you doomed my people."

"But…but I saved you," I said.

He shrugged. "Dumb luck." He waved the weapon our way. "Now go. Unless you want to join your *friend* on the floor there."

I winced as I stared at Tag, who was still smoldering, still smoking.

We all hung our heads. We walked out of the room. We walked out of the building. The food had already begun to reach the crowds. They were devouring it as we marched past them. They cheered us, not knowing they were cheering a death procession.

§ § §

We were led to a floating box. There was a large cell inside. We were thrown inside. Deadly beams contained us as we drove—and/ or floated—away.

"I'm sorry," I said to the others.

Mom held my hand. "It's always darkest before the dawn."

Craig's eyes…yeah, you know the rest. "Again, Mom, too much Hallmark Channel," he said.

She shook her head. "We saved our world. We're still together, still alive." She pointed around the cell. "Darkest," she said. She pointed to the box's wall, beyond it. "Dawn."

"More like dusk," I said.

She shrugged. "Still." She reached over and patted my hand. "Maybe the savior isn't done saving just yet."

I sighed. "Like the commander said: *dumb luck*."

And still she shrugged. "Dumb luck is still luck, Randy. And perhaps there's still enough left to go around."

I looked at Milo. He smiled. Those butterflies of mine ricocheted around my gut. "I'm with your mom here, Randy."

Cher nodded. Sonny nodded. Britney nodded. Justine Timberlake nodded—hotly. Dad nodded in double-time. Craig, well, you know what Craig did. Me, I nodded as well, if merely to make it unanimous.

Still, I was less than sure. Far, far less. As in a galaxy far, far away less. As in, I was a human who had doomed an entire race. So yeah, my nod was less than sure. In fact, my nod had no sureness left in it at all.

§§§§

We found ourselves in yet another cell after we were dropped off at yet another box of a building at the city's edge.

In bitter irony, we were fed paste and water. "What, no bread?" I deadpanned.

The guards ignored me. Stupid guards. Stupid me, too, huh? I mean, look what I'd gotten us into. I'd saved my race, but I'd condemned my family, my friends, my one-true love. Plus, Tag was dead, lying in a fried chunk in a now-deserted room. It was a horrible way to go. Then again, what way to go is any way less than horrible?

A day went by, two. We ate. We moped. I missed Tag. I felt guilty, guiltier, guiltiest.

I sat with Milo in a corner of our cell. We sat cross-legged, holding hands. "I'm sorry," I said.

He smiled. "You keep saying that."

In fact, I was on my eighty-seventh, give or take, *I'm sorry*, by that point. "I keep meaning it." I squeezed his hands. "What are your people's belief in the afterlife?"

"Such a morbid question."

I shrugged. "Humor me, please."

He sighed, and said, "In the beginning, God created the heaven and the earth. And the earth was without form, and void, and darkness was upon the face of the deep. And the Spirit of God moved upon the surface of the waters, and God said, 'let there be light,' and there was light."

"Um, yeah, I know all that already."

He smiled. "God doesn't turn off the lights, Randy."

I nodded. I got his point. I prayed my light switch got it as well. "I love you," I said.

He smiled. "You keep saying that, too."

In fact, I was on my nine-hundredth, give or take, *I love you*, by that point. "I keep meaning it." I squeezed his hands even tighter. "And I'm scared."

He turned and looked at our motley group. "Fate brought us all here for a reason, Randy. I say, just go with it."

"That easy?"

He shrugged. "Easier than the alternative."

He had a point. I had a boner. To every season turn, turn, turn. In other words, I went with it. Like he said, it was easier. And I was nothing if not easy.

§ § § §

On day three, they finally came and got us.

They lined us up. They marched us down a long white hallway. No doors. No windows. All hall. Very unnerving. Very dead-man-walking.

A wall slid open at the end of the hallway. We walked inside the room. Nine Cureans sat facing us, all of them dressed in green. That was it. Otherwise, like the hallway, everything was all white. Milo turned his face my way and whispered in my ear, "Your version of the Supreme Court. The highest court on Planet Six."

Nine utterly handsome and/or beautiful men and women stared our way. One stood and spoke in English. "You are accused of treason. How do you plead?"

I gulped. "Um, innocent?"

The one standing squinted my way. "Everything you've done, Earthling, has been captured on, as you call it, *film*. In other words, care to reconsider your plea?" He held up his hand before I could reply. "You blew up a prison. You blew up our control center. You fed the people. You pretended to be monks and nuns. You broke into several buildings, stole government ID cards, stole vehicles, stole food." He'd been reading from a list on a tablet-like device. He glanced up. "Shall I continue, Earthling?"

I gulped. I changed the subject. "You speak English quite well."

"Easy language. Picked it up in two days. We all learned it, all the judges." He sighed. He looked bored. He looked like an older version of Zac Efron. "Now then, how do you plead?"

My gulp regulped. "Innocent, but with extenuating circumstances."

"Such as?"

Such as? Such as what? What was I to do? What was I to say? I turned to my friends, my family. They merely stared back at me. I again turned to the judge. I pointed at Milo. "Love, your honor."

He smiled. Then, one by one, smiles appeared down the green line of them. "Ah," said the judge, setting the tablet down. "In that case...DEATH! Death to them all! Next case!"

"Wait! Wait!" I said.

The judge sighed. "What now, Earthling?"

What now? What now? I snapped my fingers. "I'm the savior! You can't kill the savior! I'm God's messenger." And yes, it felt both odd and douchey to utter those words. Still, what else did I have to go with.

The standing judge sat down. All nine then conversed in hushed whispers. The seconds ticked by like hours. Sweat trickle down my forehead. My heart pounded. My head pounded. My dick pounded. Then again, my dick was always pounding. I chalked it up to that Z chromosome of mine.

At last, the same judge stood. "Who, exactly, have you saved, though, Earthling?"

Fuck. "The Earth? My family? My friends?"

He nodded. "Exactly." He pointed at me. "DEATH! Death to them all!"

Fuck, yet again. Not how I thought this was supposed to go. I looked at my mom, at my dad. Where was that dawn I was promised? The darkness was here in, you know, spades. Dawn time! Hello, dawn! Only, dawn, it seemed, was still sleeping.

The guards rushed in, weapons drawn. Death. We were to be put to death. This couldn't be happening. Fate had brought us together. Fate was on our side, wasn't it? My body was trembling, hands shaking. I'd killed my friends and family as sure as if I'd put a bullet through them. Did I already say *fuck*? Because *fuck, fuck, fuck*!

A guard put his weapon to my mother's head. I started to scream, but another shout beat me to it.

"Wait!" It was Craig.

Ironically, the judge rolled his eyes. Karma, it seemed, was quite the bitch. "Please, Earthling, no more wasting our time."

"No!" shouted Craig. "I…I think I can solve all of this."

The judge glared his way. "Solve? There is nothing left to solve. The puzzle is complete. Utterly, miserably complete."

An unexpected smile spread across my brother's face. "No, sir, your honor. You're still missing a piece." He moved away from the others and approached the judges. He looked small. He looked tired. Oddly, though, his smile remained resolute. "Please, sir, just give me a minute. I promise, you will not be sorry."

"I already am, Earthling." Since he seemed to enjoy sighing, he once again did just that. "One minute, Earthling. I give you one more minute. After that—"

Craig held up his hand. "I know. DEATH! Got it, your honor. Just a minute. Promise."

He ran back our way. Surprisingly, he grabbed Britney's hand. Even more surprisingly, he kissed her, thereby using up a good twenty seconds of that measly minute. Then he whispered something into her ear. She smiled. She seemed to think whatever he said over. She nodded, her smile growing even brighter. What had he whispered to her? What could he or she possibly do now?

The minute passed. Craig returned to face the judges. He blinked. He clenched his fists. He raised his hand and pointed his index finger my way. "*He* is not the savior!"

Several gasps could be heard. Most of them came from me. "Um, what?"

He turned and faced Justin Timberlake. "You said it was fate, sir. All of this, my parents, my brother, all fated to be. My house held the portal, my mom was pregnant with Randy, the Z chromosome had to be injected into a fetus. All fate. You said it was God's will."

J.T. nodded. "I did. And it was. *Is*." He tilted his head—hotly. "And?"

Craig again turned to the judges. "The savior, your honors. It was explained to us that your people would one day venerate him. That God would not have used a slave to populate his worlds. That Adam, so to speak, must be revered. Your government was unanimous in its decision."

The judge nodded irately. "Yes, yes. So what? Like I said, like you just said, your brother is not our savior."

Craig stood there, smiling broadly. He paused, probably for effect, as that was how he rolled. Thankfully, he rocked even better. At last, he pointed at his scrawny chest. "Adam, your honors." And then he pointed at Britney. "Eve, your honors." He dropped his finger. He stood there, arms akimbo. "Randy isn't the savior, your honors…" There was that effected pause again. "Because *I* am."

Justin Timberlake rose. "Of course! I was simply a few years too early!" He nodded, you know, *hotly*. "My research has evolved these past twenty years. I can inject a Z chromosome into Britney, into the Curean female here. It will be passed down, as will the human's Y, all on our side of things, not on Earth!"

I coughed. "Wait. What?"

Justin Timberlake pointed at Craig. "He, he is the savior! His offspring with Britney will have both a Y and a Z chromosome. He will produce viable offspring." He stared at Craig. "Willingly, right?"

Craig nodded eagerly. "Definitely. Willingly. For, um, sure." He looked at Britney. "Okay with you, Brit?"

Britney nodded. "Sure. Just not right now, dude. Still got some oats to sew. Once I figure out what an oat is."

The group of them laughed. As did I. Mostly out of nerves.

"Your honors," continued J.T. "This is the prophecy. This human will be our savior, freely, of his own accord, as God would wish it. He will have children. These children will spread the Y chromosome back into our population. Our people will no longer be sterile. We will once again grow. We will once again flourish."

I smiled at Craig. Craig smiled at me. "Way to go, little bro."

"Thanks, dude," he said. "Guess I'm gonna be a daddy." To which he added, "To a whole new world."

I shrugged. "Better you than me, *dude*. Better you than me."

§ § § §

So, clearly, we were not put to DEATH!—to quote a certain judge. In fact, we were released, given our own apartments. Heck, we got our own damned building. It was a towering boxy number. No windows. No doors. At least not yet. Still, we had plans. Man, did we ever have plans.

We also had food. Lots of food. Lots of fruits and vegetables. Though I could never quite figure out which was which. As to the paste, once the people of City Northeast Nineteen had the alternative, there was no going back. Thank, you know, God.

As to my brother and Britney, they had plenty of time to repopulate the planet. Heck, they had yet to go on their first official date. Plus, they were still teenagers. Meaning, Adam and Eve had a curfew. And separate bedrooms. For now.

Justin Timberlake was given a new lab. He would ensure that my brother's Y chromosome would properly make the rounds. He also gladly accepted the role as the government's head scientist and architect, brought back from the dead, as it were. And he did all of this—last time, promise—hotly.

Mom and Dad retired. They had an entire new planet to explore, after all. Plus, they'd raised me and Craig. Meaning, they deserved a little break. And then some.

We explained to Sonny and Cher who the real Sonny and Cher were. Milo's parents, it quickly turned out, loved their music, once we played it for them. And if they could learn English in just two days, you should've seen what they could do with a bit of harmony. All that is to say, Sonny and Cher soon hit the road as, well, Sonny and Cher. On a side note, it's often been said that when the world ends, all that will be left will be Cher and cockroaches. Turned out, when a world begins, Cher will be there, too. Thankfully, the planet didn't have any bugs, just six-legged kitties.

As for me and Milo, well, now that Planet Six had an Adam and Eve, all it needed was a couple of randy snakes in the grass. And yes, randy the adjective. Big time. In other words, the people needed to learn subversion, rebellion, revolt, not to mention debauchery. A little sedition goes a long way, after all. And who better to teach them all that than us: the kings of treason—or maybe make that *queens*.

§ § § §

A month went by. We remodeled our apartment. We now had a front door, with a doorbell and everything. Nothing slid out from a wall anymore. We had furniture that wasn't made completely out of metal. We had art on the walls. We had houseplants. We didn't have any pets because, well, who wants a pet with a dozen eyes staring at you all day? Plus, all my love poured into Milo. Like a geyser. Shooting and spewing. Graphic, but true.

We were sitting in the kitchen, eating fruits and/or vegetables. We now had grains as well, rudimentary cereal. Cap'n Crunch was soon to make a major comeback. And since Cureans loved long words with impossible sounding strings of letters, Häagen-Dazs was next. Vanilla, at first, but chocolate chocolate-chip was definitely in the pipeline. Once we invented chocolate. You know, again.

The doorbell rang. I looked at Milo. "Are we expecting anyone?"

He shrugged. "My parents are on tour; yours are sailing in the southern quadrant; Craig and Britney are, well, *yuck*, I don't even want to think what those two are up to." He moved to the door. "So, no, no idea."

He opened the door. A handsome male stranger stood in the hallway. Then again, every male on the planet was handsome. Still, something about this one was especially striking. And familiar-looking.

"Can we help you?" I asked.

He nodded. He smiled. "Usually, it's the other way around, Randy."

I gasped. I recognized the voice in an instant. "But how?" I squeaked out.

He walked into the apartment—on two legs, on two feet, nothing floating, nothing see-through, nothing glowing. "Justin Timberlake designed it." He gave us a twirl. "You like?"

I ran up and hugged him. Finally! My hands wrapped around solid...well, it seemed like flesh. It even smelled like flesh—with a little cologne spritzed on for good measure. "I love it, Tag!" I pulled an inch away. "But again, how? You were burnt to a crisp, last we saw you."

"Hardware is destructible, Randy," he said. "Software is not." He smiled. I smiled. Milo smiled. "New hardware is, suffice it to say..." He tapped on his broad expanse of chest. "Indestructible. Tag 2.0, as it were. Though I like to think that I'm now a perfect ten."

"Oh brother," I said as I once again hugged him good and tight.

"Is Craig here, too?" he asked, handsome face looking left and then right.

I laughed. I laughed into his chest that smelled like cologne and flesh and wasn't the slightest bit burnt or see-through. "No, he's not," I replied. "But I have a feeling that wherever he is, his eyes are most certainly rolling."

. . . .

Thank you for taking the time to read And God Belched. *If you enjoyed it, please consider telling your friends or posting a short review. Word of mouth is an author's best friend and much appreciated. Thank you. Rob Rosen*

About the Author

Rob Rosen (www.therobrosen.com), award-winning author of the novels *Sparkle: The Queerest Book You'll Ever Love, Divas Las Vegas, Hot Lava, Southern Fried, Queerwolf, Vamp, Queens of the Apocalypse, Creature Comfort, Fate, Midlife Crisis*, and *Fierce*, and editor of the anthologies *Lust in Time, Men of the Manor, Best Gay Erotica 2015*, and *Best Gay Erotica of the Year, Volumes 1, 2 and 3*, has had short stories featured in more than 200 anthologies.

Lightning Source UK Ltd.
Milton Keynes UK
UKHW02f1838080318
319104UK00001B/4/P